Josiah Henson

Working for Freedom

The Story of Josiah Henson

Stories of Canada

Stories of Canada

Working for Freedom

The Story of Josiah Henson

by

Rona Arato

Series Editor: Allister Thompson

Napoleon Publishing

Napoleon Publishing
an imprint of Napoleon & Company
Toronto, Ontario, Canada
napoleonandcompany.com

Canadä

Napoleon & Company acknowledges the support of the Canada Council
for our publishing program.

The publication of *Working for Freedom* has been supported
by the Government of Canada through the
Book Publishing Industry Development Program.

Printed in Canada

Library and Archives Canada Cataloguing in Publication

Arato, Rona
        Working for freedom : the story of Josiah Henson / Rona Arato.

(Stories of Canada)
Includes bibliographical references and index.
ISBN 978-1-894917-50-6

        1. Henson, Josiah, 1789-1883--Juvenile literature. 2. Slaves--United
States--Biography--Juvenile literature. 3. Fugitive slaves--United
States--Biography--Juvenile literature. 4. Fugitive slaves--Canada--
Biography--Juvenile literature. 5. Blacks--Canada--Biography--Juvenile
literature. 6. Clergy--Canada--Biography--Juvenile literature.
7. Underground Railroad--Canada--Juvenile literature. I. Title. I. Series.
E444.H526A73 2008   j973.7'115092   C2008-905631-0

Table of Contents

Cruel Beginnings

An Evil Institution

Slavery formed an important part of the Southern economy. Most slaves worked on plantations, where they performed back-breaking tasks in the fields from dawn to dusk. Since slaves were not paid and were given only the barest of necessities, plantation owners were able to sell their crops for good profits. When slaves had children, those children too became slaves. Since slaves were counted as valuable property, their children added to a plantation owner's wealth.

Imagine being owned by another human being. You are that person's property, like their horse or mule. Your owner tells you when and where to work, what to wear and eat, and where to sleep. Often you do not have enough food but are made to work long hours in the scorching sun. You can be beaten for the slightest reason and sold to a new owner, so that you never see your family again.

Josiah Henson was born a slave. At that time, slavery was legal and practiced mostly in the southern United States. People were strictly divided based on the colour of their skin. White people were slave owners, and Black people were slaves. From his early years, life was hard for Josiah. With little food in his stomach, he was forced to work in the fields like an animal. Yet he rose above his cruel beginnings to become a learned and respected man.

After escaping to Canada with his family, Josiah returned south time and again, risking his life, to lead other slaves to freedom in Ontario. He helped found the town of Dawn, so that they would have a place to live, and he helped them adjust to their new lives. As slaves, they had always been told what to do; now they had to learn how to think for themselves and make their own living. Because Josiah believed that they would become independent only thorough education and skilled work, he built a sawmill, and founded Canada's first vocational school at the Dawn settlement.

African slaves were forced into crowded, unsanitary conditions on slave ships bound for the Americas.

A Slave's Life

Josiah describes his live as a slave

Like all slaves, every aspect of Josiah's life was regulated by his owner. In his autobiography, Josiah described the living conditions this way:

…The principal food consisted of corn-meal and salt herring; to which was added in summer a little buttermilk, and the few vegetables which each might raise for himself and his family. Our dress was of tow-cloth; for the children, nothing but a shirt; for the older ones, a pair of pantaloons or a gown in addition, according to the sex. In the winter a round jacket or overcoat, a wool hat once in two or three years for the males, and a pair of coarse shoes once a year.

We lodged in log huts, and on the bare ground, huddled, like cattle, ten or a dozen persons, men, women and children. Our beds were collections of straw and old rags, thrown down in the corners and boxed in with boards; a single blanket the only covering. Our favourite way of sleeping, however, was on a plank, our heads raised on an old jacket and our feet toasting before the smouldering fire. The wind whistled, and the rain and snow blew in through the cracks, and the damp earth soaked in the moisture till the floor was miry as a pig-sty. Such were our houses. In these wretched hovels were we penned at night, and fed by day; here were the children born and the sick—neglected.

Josiah Henson was born about 1789, on a Maryland plantation. His mother Celia had been hired out by her owner, Dr. McPherson, to the plantation's owner, Francis Newman. Celia met her husband on the plantation, and the couple had six children. When Josiah was still a small child, the overseer (the man in charge of the slaves) set him to work carrying buckets of water to men in the fields. Josiah's other task was to hold a horse-drawn plough that the men used for weeding between the rows of corn. As Josiah grew older and stronger, the overseer gave him a hoe and told him he was ready to do the full day's work of a man.

A family of African Americans outside former slave quarters in the early twentieth century

A. S. Seers Print. N.Y. (Copyrighted)

Life in the slave quarters was hard. Slaves lived in leaky cabins and slept on the floor with only a thin blanket for a cover. They received no money and were given only scraps of food to eat and rags to wear. Yet many of them managed to find pleasure in their families and friends, and in making music.

Josiah's father was a good-humoured and light-hearted man who often led the celebrations and fun-making in the slave quarters. He loved to strum his banjo while the others danced and sang. In spite of their slavery, Josiah's family were, for the most part, happy. Then suddenly, when Josiah was five, everything changed.

Scenes from slaves' lives, taken from the book *Uncle Tom's Cabin*

Life Changes Forever

Cruel punishment in the South

"Sold South"

Slavery was legal in the United States until the Civil War (1860-1865) brought the practice to an end. States that were south of the Mason-Dixon line (an invisible boundary between the northern state of Pennsylvania and the southern state of Maryland) were slave states. Northern states were free. For a slave in Maryland, being "sold South" meant going to a cotton plantation in a state such as Alabama, Georgia or Mississippi, where conditions were much harsher than in Maryland. Many slaves did not survive the cruel treatment and back-breaking work on these plantations. When Josiah's father was "sold South", the family knew it was a death sentence, and they would never see him again.

One day, while working in the field, Josiah's father heard his wife scream. Racing to her aid, he found the overseer attacking her. Enraged, he tore the man away from Celia and threw him to the ground. He might have killed the man were it not for his wife's hysterical pleas to stop.

At that time in Maryland, it was against the law for a Black person to strike a white person. Terrified of what would happen, Josiah's father ran away and hid in the woods. But after many days without food or water, he was forced to return to the plantation and give himself up. He was sentenced to be whipped one hundred times on his bare back and to have his right ear cut off.

On the day the sentence was carried out, Black people from the neighbouring plantations were brought in to witness the scene. It was a warning to all of them that no matter what a white person did to a Black person, the Black person must never strike back.

Josiah's father was tied to a post, and a powerful blacksmith named Hewes snapped his whip. As it sliced into his back, Josiah's father's screams could be heard a mile away. After fifty lashes, Hewes paused while a doctor checked the slave's pulse to make sure he was still alive. He might have hit a white man, but he was still a valuable piece of property, and his owner did not want him to die.

This song, which was accompanied by slaves clanking their chains, was often sung when some members of a family had been sold, leaving their loved ones behind.

When I was down in Egypt's land,
Close by the river,
I heard one tell of the promised land,
Down by the river side.

Chorus:
We'll end this strife
Down by the river,
We'll end this strife,
Down by the river side.

I never shall forget this day,
Down by the river,
When Jesus washed my sins away,
Down by the river side.

Chorus:
"Twas just before the break of day,
down by the river,
when Jesus washed my sins away,
down by the river side.

Chorus:
Cheer up, cheer up, we're gaining
ground
Down by the river.
Old Satan's kingdom we'll pull down,
Down by the river side.

Chorus:
Shout, dear children, for you are free,
Down by the river, Christ has brought to
you, liberty,
Down by the river side.

When they agreed that he would live, the blacksmith gave him the final fifty lashes. Then, as Josiah's father sagged in excruciating pain against the post, his torturer cut off his ear.

Josiah's only memory of his father was watching him come back to their cabin, his head covered with blood, while more blood streamed down his back. Although Josiah was too young to understand what had happened, he knew that it was something dreadful.

From that day on, Josiah's father sank into a deep depression that would not lift. He became sharp-tempered and surly. He would not work. When his owners could no longer tolerate his behaviour, they sold him "South" to a cotton plantation in Alabama. The family never heard from him again.

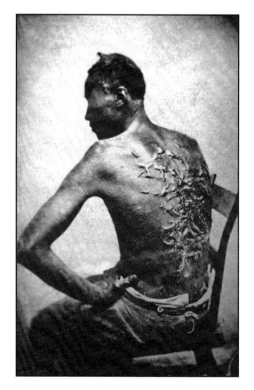

Long after slavery was abolished, the scars of cruelty were still evident.

5

The Slave Auction

Put on the block

Josiah Henson never forgot the agony of having his family sold and torn apart.

My brothers and sisters were bid off first, and one by one while my mother, paralysed by grief, held me by the hand. Her turn came, and she was bought by Isaac Riley of Montgomery County. Then I was offered to the assembled purchasers. My mother, half-distracted by the thought of parting forever from all her children, pushed through the crowd, while the bidding for me was going on, to the spot where Riley was standing. She fell at his feet and clung to his knees, entreating him in tones that only a mother could command, to buy her baby as well as herself. Will it, can it be believed that this man, thus appealed to, was capable not merely of turning a deaf ear to her supplication, but of disengaging himself from her with such violent blows and kicks, as to reduce her to the necessity of creeping out of his reach and mingling the groan of bodily suffering with the sob of a breaking heart.

After Josiah's father left, Newman returned Celia and her children to her owner, Dr. McPherson. The doctor was a kind man who treated his slaves well. He took a special liking to Celia's youngest child and gave the boy his own name, Josiah. The last name Henson was Dr. McPherson's uncle's name.

Under the doctor's tutelage, Josiah grew into a bright and curious child. Celia was a devout Christian and Josiah, following her lead, developed a strong interest in religion. For a time, the family was happy. They were together, and their master was kind. For a slave, life could get no better. Then the doctor died, and his estate, including his slaves, was sold to pay off his heirs. Josiah's entire family was to be sold at a slave auction.

Slave auctions were common in the southern United States. Plantation owners and other buyers gathered to view the slaves who, like cattle, were inspected then auctioned off to the highest bidder. Families were torn apart, in many cases never to see each other again. If a slave protested or acted up, he or she was whipped into submission. For the white southerners buying the slaves, or just coming to watch the proceedings, the auctions were part business transaction and part entertainment. For the slaves, they were a tragedy. Celia's new master was Isaac Riley, a farmer from Montgomery County. Josiah was bought by a tavern keeper named Robb who lived near the Montgomery Courthouse. Like many slave owners of the time, Robb was a cruel master who used force to intimidate his young slave. Josiah, who was

6

poorly fed and clothed, soon became ill. Robb decided he wasn't worth the money it took to keep him alive and traded him to Isaac Riley in return for free horseshoeing. Celia was ecstatic. At least she had one of her children back and, in spite of Riley's neglect and cruelty, Josiah thrived in his mother's care.

Learning to Spell

Held Back

In slaveholding states, it was illegal for Blacks to learn to read and write. Anyone caught teaching them could be prosecuted. Slave owners wanted to keep their slaves as ignorant as possible. If slaves could read, they could learn about other people living in freedom. If they could write, they could pass notes to each other about escape routes. To overcome these restrictions, many slaves developed their own verbal codes. They also used stories and songs to transmit messages whenever they could.

When Josiah was about thirteen years old, William, a slave boy from a neighbouring farm, offered to teach him how to spell. William had taught himself by listening to his master's boys talk about their lessons when he drove them to school every day in the plantation's wagon. When Josiah expressed interest, William said he would teach him, but Josiah had to buy a spelling book that cost eleven cents.

Josiah got the money by selling apples from Riley's orchard. He made ink by mixing charcoal with water and whittled a goose feather into a pointed quill. Now he had the tools he needed to learn how to write.

Josiah figured out that the letters "I" and "R" that were stamped on the blocks of butter he sold for his master stood for "Isaac Riley." At night, when he was alone, he practiced copying the letters by making squiggles in his notebook. During the day, he kept the notebook hidden under his hat.

One day, he was harnessing Riley's horse when it bolted. As he ran after it, his hat flew off, and the spelling book tumbled to the ground. At that moment, Riley appeared.

"What's that?" Riley roared, pointing to the book.

"A spelling book, Massa." As Josiah stooped to pick it up, Riley's cane smashed down on on his head. Again and again, Riley hit Josiah about the head and back until his eyes became swollen and he felt as if his body was coming apart.

"So you want to be a fine gentleman, do you?" Riley shouted as he snatched up the book. He pulled Josiah to his feet. "Remember, boy, if I catch you meddling with a book again, next time I'll knock your brains out."

Josiah did not open another book for over forty years, until he was living in freedom in Canada.

His Master's Keeper

The Riley house: no matter the size, the master's house was always called "the great house".

Slaves lacked basic legal rights

Black slaves were considered property and could be bought and sold at their owners' whim. Blacks could not own livestock, such as horses, mules, cattle or sheep. Blacks were not allowed to have any kind of weapon, and it was illegal for a Black person to ever strike a white, even in self-defence. If an owner or overseer accidentally killed a slave when disciplining him or her, that person could not be prosecuted.

Josiah did not like Riley. He found him "vulgar in his habits, unprincipled and cruel, in his general deportment and immoral." Riley was mean to his slaves and provided them with the bare minimum food they needed to stay alive. In spite of the hardships, Josiah grew up strong and healthy. His first job was as a water boy in the fields. When the overseer realized how capable Josiah was, he handed him a shovel and told him to do the same work as the grown men. By the time he was fifteen, Josiah was one of the most valuable slaves on the plantation.

He was not only physically strong, he was mentally alert. Other slaves looked up to him, and he soon became a leader. He would encourage them to work harder and longer than they had to, in hopes of getting some praise from Riley. In spite of his efforts, Riley never said a kind word to Josiah or to any of his other slaves. He did, however, appreciate that Josiah's efforts made him worth more money.

When he was eighteen, Josiah met John McKenny at church. McKenny was a white preacher who was strongly opposed to slavery. Through McKenny's influence, Josiah became a devout Christian and began preaching to other slaves.

Josiah was proud that people thought he was smart, and he worked hard to prove them right. In so doing, he set an example for others to follow. It was a pattern that he would repeat throughout his life.

Riley recognized that Josiah was honest and trustworthy. When the plantation manager quit,

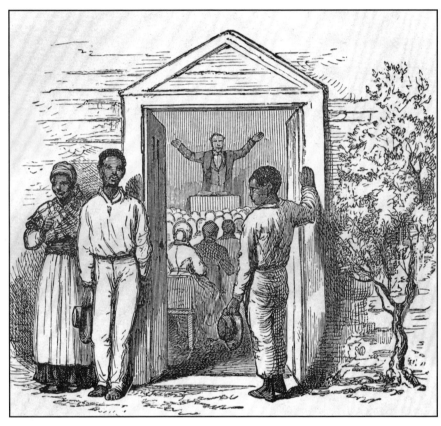

Blacks were not allowed inside the church, so they listened to the sermon from outside.

Riley gave the job to Josiah. Now Josiah had more freedom, which he used to attend church services.

Because Josiah was strong, Riley used him as a bodyguard whenever he went into town. Often on these trips, Riley drank too much liquor and become roaring drunk. One night, he got into a fight with his brother's overseer, Bruce Litton. Josiah stepped in to protect his master and, in the brawl, the overseer fell and smashed his head on the ground. Furious, the man set out to get even. A few days later, accompanied by three slaves, he caught Josiah on his way home from town and beat him up. Josiah was badly bruised, and his right arm and both shoulder blades were broken.

Although he recovered, the attack left him disabled for life. Never again could Josiah raise his hands above his shoulders. The overseer was tried for the beating, but the judge acquitted him, saying the attack was in "self-defence".

Joy and Sorrow

When Josiah was twenty-two, he married a slave girl named Charlotte, most likely in a ceremony the slaves called "Jumping the Broom". Charlotte, who belonged to a neighbouring family, was well brought up and, for a slave, very knowledgeable. Josiah was happy in his marriage and reasonably happy in his position on the plantation.

In spite of the beating he'd received, Josiah remained loyal to his master. Riley continued to rely on Josiah, whom he called Si for short, to run his plantation. Josiah, however, had no control over Riley's extravagant living habits. Eventually, his master's drinking and gambling led him into serious trouble and, at one point, Riley feared that his estate would be seized to pay for his debts. Since slaves were considered property, they too would be sold. To avoid losing them, Riley ordered Josiah to take his eighteen slaves to his brother Amos's plantation in Kentucky.

The trip itself was relatively easy. Unlike slaves from other plantations, Josiah's charges walked

Jumping the Broom

None of the slave-holding states recognized marriages between slaves as legally binding. One of the traditions the Africans brought with them was a marriage ceremony called "Jumping the Broom." This tradition had originated in Ghana. A broom symbolized sweeping away the past. It was waved over the heads of the bride and groom to ward off evil spirits. Often, the couple would jump over the broom at the end of the ceremony. Many slaves adopted this custom as a way of affirming their commitment to one another.

freely, without chains or shackles. Women and children took turns riding in the horse-drawn wagon that Riley had bought for the trip. When they reached the town of Wheeling, West Virginia, Josiah sold the wagon and bought a boat for the final lap of his journey.

To get to Kentucky, which was a slave state, the party had to cross Ohio, which was a free state. Josiah knew that he could let his charges go free. The choice tortured him. Although he loathed slavery, he felt loyal to Riley. For days he agonized over his decision. As the boat sailed through Cincinnati, free Blacks and white abolitionists (people who wanted to end slavery) lined the river banks and shouted out that Josiah and his passengers were now free.

When the boat docked in Cincinnati, crowds of free Blacks surrounded Josiah and his charges. "Why are you going on?" they shouted. "You can be your own masters and put yourselves out of reach of pursuit."

Josiah realized that the rest of his party were becoming excited with the idea of remaining free in Ohio. What was he to do? He had always yearned for freedom but had planned to buy it, not run away. He had promised to take Riley's property to Kentucky and believed that that was what he must do. He told the boat captain to push away from the shore and continue the journey down river.

As the boat moved forward, the people on shore showered Josiah with curses. Josiah's charges, however, were so used to following orders, they never questioned his decision.

Josiah delivered all eighteen, as promised, to Riley's brother Amos. It was an act he would regret for the rest of his life.

A New Home

The Fugitive Slave Act

In 1793 the United States passed the Fugitive Slave Act, which allowed anyone to capture an escaped slave. Many free Black people were picked up, but they could appeal to a federal district or circuit judge or any state magistrate to decide on their status, without a jury trial.

Southern slaveholders felt that the Fugitive Slave Act was too lenient. In 1850, they pressured the federal government to pass the Second Fugitive Slave Act. It stated that anyone even suspected of being a runaway slave could be arrested without a warrant and turned over to any person who swore that he/she was the slave's owner. A captured Black person, even one who had been born free in the North, could not ask for a jury trial nor testify on his or her own behalf. Canada became the only place that was truly safe for an escaped slave.

The cover to sheet music of a song about Frederick Douglass, a famous abolitionist and escaped slave

The conditions on Amos Riley's Kentucky plantation were better than those Josiah and his charges had left behind. The plantation was large and fertile, and there was ample food and decent shelter. Josiah became superintendent over a hundred other slaves.

Josiah found that people in Kentucky had more liberal attitudes towards slaves than the people he had known in Maryland. He took advantage of his position as superintendent to attend local church services. Josiah found that by attending white services, he was able to broaden his knowledge of Christianity. His faith deepened as he accepted the moral precepts, and he learned how to transfer his enthusiasm to those around him. Once again, as he had back in Maryland with John McKenny, Josiah began preaching to the slaves on the plantation. Josiah was recognized as a preacher by the Conference of the Methodist Episcopal Church and became popular with both Black and white congregations.

Josiah stayed on Amos Riley's plantation for three years, waiting for Isaac Riley to move with his family to Kentucky. But in the spring of 1828, Riley sent word that, because his wife refused to go with him, he was forced to remain in Maryland. He would, therefore, have to sell all his slaves, with the exception of Josiah, his wife and their four children.

Josiah was devastated. By refusing to free his charges in Cincinnati, he had

Holy Bible
Thou shalt deliver unto the master his servant which has escaped from his master unto thee. He shall dwell with thee. Even among you in that place which he shall choose in one of thy gates where it liketh him best. Thou shalt not oppress him
Deut XXIII.15, 16.

Effects of the Fugitive-Slave-Law.

Declaration of Independence
We hold that all men are created equal; that they are endowed by their Creator with certain unalienable rights that among these are life, liberty, and the pursuit of happiness.

Entered according to Act of Congress in the year 1850 by M.B. and Dodo in the Clerks Office of the District Court of the Southern District of New York.

This illustration is a protest against the Fugitive Slave Act.

doomed them to the horror of being sold South. Once again, he was forced to watch the ordeal of a slave auction. People he had lived with and valued as friends had their lives torn apart. Josiah agonized as husbands and wives were separated; mothers were pulled away from their children, and children separated from brothers and sisters. The people who bought and sold them cared no more about their feelings than if they had been cattle. Josiah's hatred of slavery and everyone involved in keeping it alive grew.

Riley kept Josiah and his family because he wanted to bring them back to Maryland. In the three years that Josiah was on Amos's plantation, Isaac Riley's fortunes had fallen to desperate levels. Most of his land was gone, and he had to hire help to till the bits of land he still owned. A tug of war developed. Amos wanted to keep Josiah because he saved him the cost of hiring an overseer, and Isaac wanted Amos to give Josiah a pass that would allow him to travel through other southern states and return to Maryland. Without the pass, he could be picked up at any time and sold South, under the terms of the Fugitive Slave Act.

Josiah waited on the sidelines while the brothers battled about his fate. He was afraid to let them see how badly he wanted that pass, because Josiah had a plan, and he needed the pass to achieve it.

Josiah's Plan

A Servant, Not a Slave

The certificate that Amos Riley gave Josiah said he was a "servant" of Amos Riley—not a slave. As a servant, Josiah could travel as a free man without the restrictions that his slave status would have imposed on him. In his autobiography, Josiah talks about the way he was treated once he was off the plantation.

…Everywhere I went, I was met by kindness. The contrast between the respect with which I was treated and the ordinary abuse of plantation life gratified me in the extreme, as it must anyone who has within him one spark of personal dignity as a man.

Josiah had become a popular preacher who was often invited to speak in white churches. In the summer of 1828, he met a Methodist preacher who took an interest in him. One day, the man took Josiah aside and told him, "You ought to be free. You have too much capacity to be confined to the limited and comparatively useless sphere of a slave."

Josiah listened with interest as the man set out a plan. Josiah was to go to Mr. Amos and get his consent to visit his brother Isaac Riley in Maryland. "Then," the man continued, "I will try and put you in a way by which I think you may succeed in buying yourself."

Josiah was thrilled. Imagine securing his freedom! His problem was how to approach Amos without arousing his suspicion.

Josiah brought up the idea of going to Maryland on a Sunday morning as he was shaving Amos. Josiah wet his brush and worked up a rich lather from the bar of soap he held in his left hand. As he lathered the lower half of Amos's face, Josiah began to speak. "You know, Mr. Amos, I've been thinking. It sure has been a long time since I was on the plantation, and I would like to see my master, Mr. Riley, again." He pressed the shaving brush against the other man's mouth, so Amos couldn't respond until he had finished. "I don't want to make any hardship for you, sir, but if you could spare me for awhile…"

Amos waited until Josiah wiped the soap from his face. Then he sat up and swivelled around so he was facing his slave.

"Why, Josiah, I think you've earned the right to visit your home plantation. You've been a big help to me these past three years."

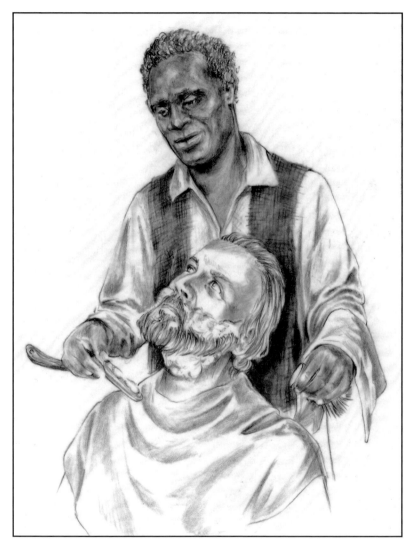

Josiah stared at Mr. Amos in surprise. He had expected an argument, and instead he was getting permission.

Mr. Amos said he liked and trusted Josiah and told him that he had worked hard and earned the privilege. He gave Josiah a certificate that said he was a servant of Amos Riley and had Mr. Riley's permission to pass back and forth between Kentucky and Maryland. Josiah's Methodist friend gave him a letter of recommendation. In September of 1828, Josiah left the plantation and set out to put his plan in motion.

He left Charlotte and the children on the plantation with the hope that once he attained his own freedom, he could work to free them as well.

Powerful Friends

Buying Freedom

Slaves could obtain freedom in one of several ways. A master could grant a slave his or her freedom. In some rare cases, slaves could buy their own freedom. Although slaves were never paid for their labours, a few, such as Josiah, were allowed to earn money outside of the plantation. A master would set a freedom price, and when a slave had the money, the master would take it in return for manumission papers stating that the person in question was free. The freed slave had to carry these papers at all times. Without them, Blacks, even those born free in the northern states, could be captured by bounty hunters and sold South.

A Black preacher

In Cincinnati, Josiah met a sympathetic man who introduced him to influential people who became his friends. Many of them were abolitionists who wanted to see slavery outlawed. For the first time in his life, Josiah was free to speak his mind and tell people what he really thought. What a joy! People looked up to him, not as a slave, but as a man of substance and passion. All over Ohio, Josiah preached and people listened as he spoke from his heart about the evils of slavery.

In Ohio, Josiah was free. He could move about as he pleased and eat whatever he wanted, whenever he felt like eating. At last he could look directly into people's eyes when he addressed them. Flushed with this new freedom, he held his head high, threw his shoulders back and walked with the confident stride of a free man. The more he experienced the miracle of his own emancipation, the more Josiah became convinced that slavery was a cruel and immoral institution that had to be abolished.

Josiah was also discovering that he was a natural born speaker. People paid to hear him. After only six days of preaching in Cincinnati, he had $160 in his pocket. By the time he left Ohio for Maryland, several weeks later, he had $275 in cash, a fine horse and a new suit of clothes. Josiah was ready to buy his freedom from Riley.

A Rude Awakening

"Josiah!" Riley ran down the steps of the great house, waving his arms and shouting with joy. "What a great surprise. You're back."

Josiah sat astride his horse and watched as Riley greeted him. Could it be, he thought, that his master was actually happy to see him? Josiah smiled, then pressed his heels into the horse's side and trotted up to the house.

"Good day, Master Riley," he said, as he dismounted and landed lightly on the ground.

Riley looked up at Josiah, and his welcoming smile turned to a scowl. All at once, Josiah pictured himself as Riley saw him—tall, elegantly groomed, self-composed and riding a fine horse. The slave, Josiah realized, looked better than the master. The past three years had not been kind to Riley. The plantation was run down; the house needed paint, and all the slaves had either been sent to Mr. Amos or sold off. Riley himself was dressed in shabby clothes that needed a good wash.

Josiah's Pass

By taking away Josiah's certificate, Riley was asserting his authority over his slave. Josiah's appearance and manner offended Riley, because Josiah made Riley realize how far his own fortunes had fallen. Riley was a drunkard and had ruined his plantation through neglect. Because he was white, however, he was still superior to Josiah in his own eyes and those of the law. By taking his slave's paper, he wanted to make it clear to Josiah who was the boss.

This famous image was the seal of the Society for the Abolition of Slavery in England.

Riley's initial excitement turned sour. How dare Josiah put on airs! Why, the slave's clothes were far better than those he himself wore! He glared at Josiah with a look that seemed to say, "I'll take the gentleman out of you soon enough."

Josiah tied his horse to a post and stepped forward.

"Where'd you get that horse?" Riley pointed at Josiah's clothes. "And them duds? You think you're a gentleman or something?"

Josiah took a deep breath. "I earned the money to buy the horse and my clothes by preaching to congregations in Ohio."

"People pay you to preach?" Riley snorted with laughter. "What else they pay you to do? And how did you get here? Do you have a pass?" Riley demanded.

"Yes, sir, I do." Josiah showed him the paper that Mr. Amos had given him.

Riley snatched the pass from Josiah's hand and gave it to his wife, who was hovering behind him. "Lock this in the top drawer of my desk. For safekeeping," he said, turning back to Josiah.

Josiah stood still as a stone. He felt as if a cell door had slammed behind him, locking him into a prison from which he had only recently escaped. Before arriving at the plantation, he had been a proud free man. Then, with a few words from Riley, he had once again been reduced to the status of a grovelling slave.

To Win His Freedom

The fireplace in Riley's house in front of which Josiah slept, as it looks today. The house is now a museum.

"I will not let him defeat me," Josiah vowed as he led his horse across the yard to the stable. The further he went into the plantation, the deeper his spirits sank. Riley's farm was in terrible shape. Paint peeled off the front of the house, and the fields were barren of crops. Riley had sold the few slaves that had not gone to Kentucky with Josiah, and the hired hands that replaced them were slovenly and destitute. The entire plantation reeked of poverty. Even Riley, Josiah thought, looked like he was on the brink of collapse.

After tending to his horse, Josiah returned to the kitchen. The inside of the house was as run down as the exterior. Looking around, he sighed. After his first exuberant greeting, Riley had resumed his bullying ways.

"You sleep here, with the hired help," Riley said, pointing to the dirt floor in front of the soot clogged fireplace.

That night, as he lay on his back, Josiah thought about the hopelessness of life as a slave. While travelling in the free states, he had slept on real beds in proper bedrooms with fine linens and solid wood floors. Now, once again he was lying on a mud floor in a crowded room with no mattress or pillow and only a thin blanket for a

Free States and Slave States

The United States was divided between free and slave-holding states. The northern states such as New York, Pennsylvania and Ohio were free. The eleven southern states, including Georgia, Mississippi, Maryland and South Carolina, were slave states. The South had a mostly agricultural economy and used slaves to work on the farms and plantations. The North was mostly industrial, and the Blacks living there were free.

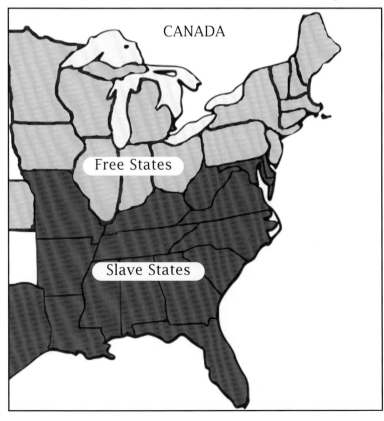

cover. A fog of depression rolled over him. His mother had died in his absence, and there was no one among the snoring men who shared his sleeping quarters that he knew or cared about. Yet even as his spirits sank, Josiah's determination to buy his freedom burned stronger than ever. "I have not come this far to spend the rest of my life tending to Riley's drunken needs," he vowed. But he knew he must be careful not to give Riley any clues to his plan.

Josiah remained awake all that night, thinking about what he could do. He felt trapped and helpless. Then he thought of the one person who could help him—Riley's brother-in-law, "Master Frank". Josiah had befriended Frank when he was a young boy living in Riley's home. When Riley had abused and mistreated the lad, Josiah had treated him kindly. Now a grown man, Frank was a successful businessman living in Washington, D.C., the capital of the United States. Josiah decided to go to him and ask for help. But first he had to get his travel pass back from Riley. And he had to do it without giving Riley a single clue as to the true purpose of his trip.

A Visit to Master Frank

Washington D.C., Capital of the United States

Philadelphia was the first capital of the United States, but the country's founders wanted to build a new city that would be separate from all of the thirteen states. Two of the nation's founders, Thomas Jefferson and Alexander Hamilton, agreed that the capital should be in the south. The states of Maryland and Virginia each gave land, which totalled one hundred square miles, to form the new district.

For the city centre, which would house the government buildings, the new country's first president, George Washington, chose a site on the Potomac River, because he thought the waterway would make a good transportation route. He called the district Federal City. Later, federal commissioners named the city centre Washington and called the entire area the District of Columbia.

The White House was the first building erected in the new capital. The cornerstone was laid on October 13, 1792, the day after the country celebrated the first Columbus Day, marking the 300th anniversary of Columbus's voyage to the New World.

The next morning, Josiah waited until Riley had left for his daily visit to the local tavern. Then he saddled his horse and rode up to the house. Mrs. Riley came out on the steps to look at his horse. "Where are you going, Si?"

"I am going to Washington to see Master Frank," Josiah said, "and I must take my pass with me, if you please."

Mrs. Riley looked up at him and smiled. "Everyone knows you here, Si," she said. "You won't need your pass."

Josiah shook his head. Keeping his voice steady, he explained that were he to go to Washington without it, he might be stopped by a stranger who would harass him or attack him physically. He could not take that chance.

Many of the labourers who built the White House were slaves.

"In that case, I will get it for you." Mrs. Riley went into the house and returned with the pass in her hand.

Josiah took it and sighed with relief. The first part of his plan had worked. He had his pass, and Mrs. Riley had not guessed the real reason for his journey. He turned his horse and headed for Washington.

"Josiah! How good to see you. My word, you are such a gentleman." Frank shook his hand and smiled

warmly. "What brings you to Washington?" he said as he led Josiah into the house.

The two men settled into chairs in Frank's parlour. Josiah brought him up to date on his past three years. He and Charlotte had four children, he said. He told Frank about his preaching in Ohio, and his trip to Riley's plantation.

"I have some money," Josiah said. "I want to use it to buy my emancipation."

Frank listened attentively. He had known Josiah all his life. He remembered that when Riley had abused him as a child, Josiah had treated him kindly. Josiah was smart, loyal and brave. He took the other man's hand. "You deserve your freedom, Josiah. I will gladly help you."

As they continued talking, Josiah learned that Frank hated Riley almost as much as he did. Riley had cheated Frank out of property he had held in trust for Frank as his guardian.

"I will go to Riley and negotiate a price for your freedom," Frank promised as they stood.

Josiah sighed with relief. His dream was now much closer to becoming a reality.

23

Manumission Papers

Manumission

Manumission papers were given to slaves at the time they were freed. The paper was signed by the former owner of the slave and certified that the African-American holding the paper was a free man or woman. In theory, the manumission paper protected the former slave against capture under the Fugitive Slave Laws. Since African-Americans could not testify in court and had little legal standing even in the North, the manumission paper testified for them. Manumission papers also protected the former owner from certain obligations under the abolition laws of New York. In New York, former slave owners were required to provide for the continued welfare of their former slaves for a period of time.

Most often, manumission papers were recorded by the town clerk in the town where the slave was freed. That was usually the place where the former owner lived. Manumission papers were often recorded in unusual places within the clerk's records.

A few days after Josiah's visit, Master Frank rode to Riley's plantation. Once there, he sat down with Riley to talk about Josiah. "Josiah has saved some money, and he wants to buy his freedom," said Frank. "He has served this family faithfully for many years. Josiah is smart," he continued. "He has money, a horse and his pass. If you refuse to deal with him now, he will find a way to free himself, and then you will lose both Josiah and his money."

Riley frowned. He didn't want to give Josiah his freedom, yet what Frank said was true. Now that Josiah had his pass back, he could travel anywhere he wanted to go. And besides, Riley needed the money. Riley agreed to give Josiah his manumission papers for $450—$350 of it in cash and the remaining $100 in a promissory note.

Josiah was elated when he heard the news. Between the cash he had left and his horse, he could meet Riley's price. He would soon be a free man. The blanket of despair that had covered him since arriving at Riley's disappeared. His future would be his own.

Josiah stayed at Riley's plantation until all the plans for his freedom were completed. He received his manumission papers on March 9, 1829 and immediately prepared to return to Kentucky.

The next morning, as he was getting ready to leave, Riley approached him. "So, Josiah, now that you are a free man. What are your plans? What will you do with your certificate of freedom? Will you show it on the road as you travel?"

"Yes, sir, I will."

"You'll be a fool if you do that. Some slave trader will get hold of it and tear it up. You'll be thrown into prison and sold before any of your friends can help you."

Josiah listened to Riley. The man had a valid point. Josiah had heard of these things happening to other freed slaves.

"Don't show your papers at all," Riley continued. "Your pass is enough. Let me put your papers into a sealed envelope addressed to my brother. No one will break the seal for that is a state prison matter, an offence for which one can be sent to jail. That way, when you arrive in Kentucky, you will have it safe and sound."

This seemed like a sensible plan to Josiah. He gave his papers to Riley, who enclosed them in an envelope which he addressed and secured with three wax seals. Riley handed the envelope to Josiah, who stowed it in his carpetbag with his other possessions.

An example of manumission papers

Betrayed!

Josiah, now without his horse, began his journey on foot. When, after several days, he reached the town of Wheeling, he boarded a boat for Kentucky. Several times during his journey, he was arrested as a runaway slave, but because his pass from Amos was legitimate, he always convinced the authorities to release him.

After he left the boat in Louisville, Kentucky, Josiah walked the last five miles home. There was a spring in his step. Tired as he was from the long journey, he was filled with a joy such as he had never before known. He was returning to Amos's plantation as a free man. Everywhere he looked, the world seemed fresh and new. Even the air tasted better as he breathed in the scents of sun-warmed grass and wild flowers.

When he reached the plantation, Josiah went straight to his own cabin. He could hardly wait to see Charlotte and tell her his good news.

"Josiah, you're home!" Charlotte hugged him, and his children danced around his legs in excitement.

As Josiah related his adventures, Charlotte interrupted him. Mr. Amos had received letters from a number of people telling him of Josiah's accomplishments. "The children of the family were happy to tell us how you were preaching and making money and bargaining for your freedom." Charlotte stopped and looked at her husband, hands on hips, her head tilted to one side. "How did you raise the money?"

"I earned it preaching," Josiah said.

"Whew," Charlotte breathed. "I thought maybe you stole it."

Josiah threw back his head and laughed. "Listen here, woman, don't you trust me?"

Charlotte took a step back and looked up at him. "Josiah, how much money did you earn?"

"I paid Riley $350."

"How are you going to pay him the rest of the thousand dollars?"

PICKING COTTON ON A GEORGIA PLANTATION.

"What thousand dollars?"

"The thousand dollars you owe Mr. Riley for your manumission papers."

Josiah stared at her in horror.

Charlotte continued. "Master Amos said you paid the $350 down, and when you make up the rest of the $1,000, you will get your papers."

Once again Josiah felt as if a cell door had slammed in his face. The blood pounded in his ears. Riley's infamy was clear to him now. He had sealed the papers, so that Josiah wouldn't learn of his deception until it was too late to protest. What could Josiah do? His only ally, Master Frank, was a thousand miles away. He couldn't write to him, because like all slaves, he could neither read nor write. And there was no one he could ask, because the only people who knew how to write were slave owners. If he complained to a magistrate, he would be seized and "sold down the river." His heart, which, on his way home had been bursting with joy, became so heavy, he thought it would drop right out of this chest.

Josiah made a quick decision. "I haven't seen my papers since I left Louisville," he told Charlotte. "If you should happen to go through my bag and find them, don't tell me. Just put them somewhere far away, where I won't see them." With a sigh, he sank onto a chair and put his head in his hands. Riley, he now knew, would never let him go. What was he going to do?

27

Down the River

New Orleans

New Orleans, which is located on the Mississippi River, is the largest city in the southern state of Louisiana. During the years of the slave trade, New Orleans was an important port where slaves were bought and sold.

In 1808, the United States outlawed the practice of importing slaves from Africa. Slaves already in the country, however, were often moved from one place to another, and many were sold South. When the slaves arrived in New Orleans, a customs officer checked to make sure that none of them had been imported. Even though they were born in America, the slaves did not have any of the rights and privileges of United States citizens.

Josiah's grief and anger over Riley's betrayal threatened to overwhelm him. Forcing himself to put it from his mind, he continued his duties for Amos and took what joy he could from the comfort of his family. Life progressed in this manner for about a year. Then one day, Amos informed Josiah that his twenty-one year old son, also called Amos, was taking a flat-bottomed boat filled with farm produce down the river to New Orleans. Riley ordered Josiah to accompany the younger Amos on the trip.

Josiah knew what this meant. After all his years of loyalty to Riley and his brother, the two men had decided to sell him. Yet what could he do? He was a slave, and slaves had no choice but to go where their masters sent them.

"There is one thing I want you to do for me," he told Charlotte as they sat in their cabin a few days before his departure. "Sew my manumission papers securely into a piece of cloth then sew that again around my person. Maybe they can yet save me."

On the day he was to leave, Josiah bid a heart-rending farewell to Charlotte and his children; he knew that he might never see them again. Then he boarded the boat with Amos, the captain and four crew members and, with a last mournful look at the shore, set off for New Orleans.

On the trip down the river, the boat stopped at Vicksburg, Mississippi. Josiah asked for and received permission to visit a nearby

A Mississippi River steamboat

28

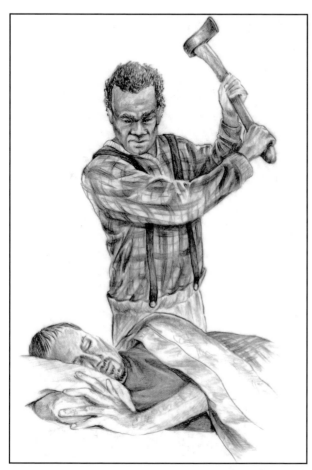

plantation, where some of the slaves he had brought from Riley's place who had been sold South were now living. The visit horrified him. Four years of working under inhuman conditions for a tyrannical master had reduced his friends to walking skeletons. They told Josiah of their daily life—toiling half-naked under a broiling sun in marshes swarming with mosquitoes and black gnats.

"Our only hope for deliverance," said one of the men, "is to die."

"You are going to the same fate, Josiah," said a woman, tears streaming down her sunken cheeks.

Josiah returned to the boat sick at heart. His decision to deliver these slaves rather than free them in Ohio had doomed them, just as Riley's treachery was now dooming him.

Back on the boat, Josiah brooded over his fate. That night, while everyone else was asleep, he decided that his only chance at freedom was to kill everyone on board and escape. Grabbing an axe, he climbed down into the hold. As he raised his weapon to strike Amos, who was sound asleep, reality washed over him like raging storm.

"My God, what am I doing?" he thought. "What! Commit murder! And you a Christian!" he told himself. Lowering the axe, he climbed back to the deck. He had deluded himself that he was acting in self-defence. Even in his desperate situation, he could not murder another human being.

Now he could only wait to see what his fate would be when he and his party reached New Orleans.

Saved!

In New Orleans, the younger Amos sold the produce on his boat and arranged to have the boat broken up. Then he prepared to board a steamship for the trip home. One task remained: to sell Josiah.

Josiah knew that young Amos was not happy with the prospect of selling him. Amos's conscience was troubling him, because he knew that what he was doing was cruel and wicked. In hopes of changing his mind, Josiah confronted him, falling to his knees and begging him to relent. Amos, however, was not to be moved. To him Josiah was not really a man, a father and a husband, but valuable property to be bought and sold. He would obey his father's order.

A contemporary painting of New Orleans in 1852

The night before the sale, Josiah could not sleep. Pictures of Charlotte and the children passed before his eyes. He thought of his mother's agonized pleas as her children were torn from her arms. Was he never to see his wife and children again? And what would happen to them? Would they too be sold South? The thought was too awful to bear. As the hours crept by, Josiah's misery increased. Then, shortly before dawn, Amos called him.

"My stomach is disordered," said Amos.

"You should lie down; it will soon pass," Josiah responded.

As the morning progressed, however, Amos's

Slave Manifests

A ship's manifest is the list of the cargo it is carrying. In New Orleans, slave ships carried manifests listing the names and characteristics of the people on board. A customs official checked the manifest then examined each slave to make sure he or she matched the description. Then he wrote a report on each. Many of the descriptions dealt with the slave's degree of blackness, for example:

1. George Washington appears not to be quite black. I should judge him to be three fourths, or, if such a mixture be possible, four-fifths black.

2. James Brown appeared to have a tawny tinge instead of black; but which, I conceive, might be the effect of ill health.

3. Sam White appears to be a full-blooded mulatto, but in other respects agrees with his description in the manifest.

condition worsened. Josiah realized that he was suffering from a condition called river fever. It was a serious disease common in New Orleans' hot, humid, mosquito-infested air. Josiah realized that Amos's affliction could become his own salvation. Amos, terrified of dying, and writhing with pain, forgot about selling Josiah and clung to him as his only friend in a strange city. To Amos, the illness was a terrifying battle for his life. For Josiah, it was a miracle. As he tended to the young man, Josiah could not believe his luck. He was saved! He was sure that Amos could not sell him now.

The ship's manifest of a slave trading vessel. Each line is the name of a slave and his or her details.

31

Land of Hope

Why did escaped slaves look to Canada as their best hope for freedom? Once they reached northern states, such as Pennsylvania or New York, they were technically free. However, even in the North, they feared bounty hunters, who were constantly on the lookout for slaves they could capture and return to the South for rewards. Canada, however, was a different country, where slavery was outlawed. Once across the border, escaped slaves could build new lives, without fear of being captured and, once again, sold South.

Canada: Land of Freedom

Josiah and Amos arrived home on July 10, 1830. Amos told everyone that, if not for Josiah, he would have died. It was the only time he mentioned the incident. Both the elder and younger Rileys treated Josiah as if nothing had happened. Josiah, however, suspected that they thought that the resourcefulness he had shown in helping young Amos, had made him stronger and, therefore, worth more money. He believed the brothers would again try to sell him.

During his travels in Ohio, Josiah had learned that the only truly safe place for an escaped slave was Canada. He had met people called Abolitionists who helped fleeing slaves through a network known as the Underground Railroad. Knowing that Riley was still planning to sell him, Josiah decided it was time to escape. His challenge was to convince Charlotte to leave with him.

"We shall die in the wilderness; we shall be hunted down with bloodhounds; we shall be brought back and whipped to death," she cried when Josiah told her of his plan. "Please, Josiah, stay home and be content."

Over and over, Josiah pleaded with her. He did not want to live as a slave any more; he wanted freedom for himself and his family. But Charlotte was a timid woman with no knowledge of the outside world. Finally, in desperation, Josiah told her: "I would hate to do it, but if you don't come with me, I will take the children and leave without you."

The following morning, as he was leaving for his daily farm chores, Charlotte ran out of the cabin after him. With tears streaming down her face, she clutched Josiah's arm. "I will go with you."

32

The biggest problem now, as Josiah saw it, was how to carry the two youngest of his four children, who were only two and three years old. He asked Charlotte to sew a knapsack with strong thick straps that slipped over his shoulders. Josiah tested it by carrying the children outside at night. When he was certain he could hold them, he made his plans.

Josiah decided to leave the following Saturday night. Sunday was a holiday. On Monday and Tuesday, he was supposed to be working on a distant farm, so he would not be missed until Wednesday. By then, he reasoned, he and his family would be far enough away to escape capture.

One task remained. Josiah's oldest son, Tom, was working in the great house with Amos. Josiah needed to get his permission for Tom to come home.

That night he went to see Amos and report on his work. As he was leaving, he turned and said, "Master Amos, I 'most forgot. Tom's mother wants to know if you won't let him come down a few days; she wants to mend his clothes and fix him up a little."

"Yes, boy, yes; he can go," said Amos.

"Thankee, Master Amos; good night, good night. The Lord bless you," said Josiah. Inwardly he laughed as he thought of just how long a goodbye it was going to be.

Josiah had arranged for a fellow slave to ferry them across the river in a small boat. From there they would proceed on foot. All the plans were now in place. So on Saturday, in the deep of night, when everyone on the farm was asleep, Josiah and his family finally left their place of bondage.

Escape

The Drinking Gourd

Slaves fleeing to freedom knew they had to go north. Because their owners kept them illiterate, they had little knowledge of geography. They did, however, know about the North Star, named Polaris, which is in the Big Dipper, part of Ursa Major, the Great Bear constellation. That star became their symbol of freedom. Because of the Big Dipper's shape (like a hollowed out gourd used for dipping into water) they called it "the drinking gourd".

Blacks brought a tradition of music with them from Africa. They coded songs to transmit messages they did not want whites to hear. The popular folk song "Follow the Drinking Gourd" provided slaves with an escape route from Alabama and Mississippi. They learned the route from a man called Peg Leg Joe, a carpenter who went from plantation to plantation teaching slaves how to escape to freedom.

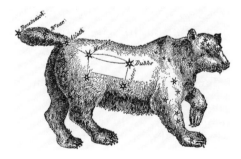

By nine o'clock on Saturday night, the Hensons were ready to leave. It was mid September, a moonless night. Silently, the family made their way to the river and climbed into the boat. No one said a word. They barely breathed. When they reached the middle of the river, Josiah's friend turned to him.

"It will be the end of me if this is ever found out, but you won't be brought back alive, Si, will you?"

Josiah shook his head. "Not if I can help it." He thought of the pistols and a knife he had bought. He hoped he wouldn't have to use them, but if it meant his family's lives, he would.

"And if you're seized, you'll never tell my part in this business?

"Not if I'm shot through like a sieve," Josiah assured him.

They rowed on until they reached the shore. They were now in Indiana, a free state, but they were still not out of danger. Josiah knew that people in the area were bitterly opposed to fugitives and, if caught, he and his family would be thrown into jail. There were only a few hours of darkness left for them to reach the woods, where they would hide during the day.

As darkness fell on the following day, they began their trek. The two older boys walked with Charlotte while Josiah carried the little ones on his back. He was strong from years of work on the plantation, yet his body soon ached from the load. Every step posed a threat. There could be animals waiting to pounce on them or bounty hunters listening for twigs snapping under their feet. When they stopped to rest the first morning, Charlotte was trembling.

The song:
"Follow the Drinking Gourd"

When the Sun comes back
And the first quail calls
Follow the Drinking Gourd.
For the old man is a-waiting for to carry
you to freedom
If you follow the Drinking Gourd.

The riverbank makes a very good road.
The dead trees will show you the way.
Left foot, peg foot, traveling on,
Follow the Drinking Gourd.

The river ends between two hills
Follow the Drinking Gourd.
There's another river on the other side
Follow the Drinking Gourd.

When the great big river meets the little river
Follow the Drinking Gourd.
For the old man is a-waiting for to carry
you to freedom
If you follow the drinking gourd.

"How could you bring us into such misery?" she scolded her husband. "Please, Josiah," she begged him. "We must turn back."

Josiah frowned. "We cannot do that, Charlotte. We have to continue."

Cold, hungry and exhausted, they slogged on for the next two weeks, walking at night and hiding in the woods during the day. As they walked, Josiah looked to the North Star, which slaves called the Drinking Gourd, to guide them. He wanted to get to Cincinnati, where his friends would help.

Josiah was terrified of being caught and often woke with his heart pounding. His shoulders and back ached from carrying the two children. His legs were like wood. The supplies they had brought were running out, and at night the children cried with hunger. Finally, Josiah decided he must find food.

At dawn, he left his family and walked until he saw a house. The owner refused to help. The same thing happened at the next house, but at the third he met a kindly woman.

She led Josiah into the kitchen and filled a plate with venison and bread. Josiah scraped the food into a large handkerchief. When he tried to pay her, she handed the money back and gave him more food. "God bless you," she said.

Tears streaming down his face, Josiah thanked her and headed back to the woods. After eating, the children were thirsty, so Josiah found a small stream, filled both his shoes with water and brought it back to them. "Of all the drinks I've ever had," he thought, "nothing has tasted as good as the water from this stream."

The next day, they travelled a great distance, and two days later, the family reached Cincinnati.

35

The Underground Railroad

The Underground Railroad was the name given to the abolitionist network that helped slaves escape to freedom. It took its name from the new railroads that were being built throughout the the United States and Canada. It began towards the end of the 1700s and lasted until the close of the Civil War in 1865. People who helped escaping slaves were called "conductors". Homes and businesses where runaways could rest and get food were called "stations" and "depots" and were run by "stationmasters". Stations were about twenty miles apart.

Stationmasters often placed lit candles in a window or lanterns in the front yard as a signal to runaways. Escaping slaves travelled by night, moving silently through the forest. They often went without food or shelter for days on end before they reached a depot. Many were caught.

The Underground Railroad was made up of many individuals, whites and free Blacks. It is estimated that by 1850, approximately 3,000 people worked on the Underground Railroad. They provided money, food, clothing, the names of other sympathizers, transportation and hope. The various routes went through fourteen northern states to Canada. In spite of its lack of a central organization and the danger faced by everyone involved, the Railroad moved thousands of slaves to freedom.

A Long and Dangerous Journey

When they reached Cincinnati, Josiah hid Charlotte and the children in the woods and walked into town to find his friends, the people he had stayed with on his trip from Kentucky to Maryland. They were delighted to see him and were quick to offer help. He went back for his family.

For the next week, the Hensons recovered from their journey in their friends' home. During the day they rested and ate nourishing food: porridge, soups, meat, potatoes and fresh-baked bread. At night they slept in real beds with feather pillows and warm wool blankets. When they felt strong enough to travel, their friends put them into a wagon and drove thirty miles to a spot where, they told the family, it was safe to resume their trip on foot.

Once again, the Hensons rested in the woods by day and travelled at night until they reached a road they had been told was safe to travel in daylight. As they moved forward, Josiah realized the road cut through a vast wilderness. Fallen trees blocked their path. The ground was rocky. There was nothing edible for them to pick, and no houses where they could get food or water. For two days they trudged through the woods, cold, hungry, and exhausted.

Towards the end of the second day, Josiah was a few feet ahead of his family, seeking a way through the underbrush, when he heard his children scream.

"Mama's dead," his son called out.

Josiah whirled around and raced back to where

the children crowded around Charlotte, who was slumped on the ground.

Josiah gently turned her over. Her skin was clammy, and he had trouble finding her pulse. "Charlotte, please, Charlotte, wake up."

After a few minutes, Charlotte moaned, and her eyelids fluttered open. Josiah lifted her and propped her head against his chest.

"Papa, is Mama alive?" his daughter whispered.

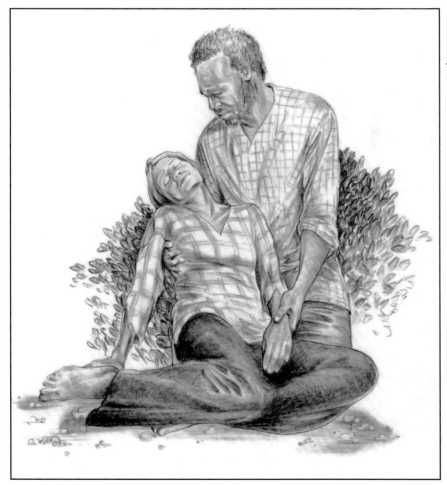

"She's alive, but barely," Josiah said. Reaching into his jacket, he pulled out a small chunk of dried beef—the last of the family's food. He broke off a piece and slipped it between Charlotte's lips. She was so weak, she could barely chew. Slowly, gently, he fed her the meat until she regained enough strength to stand.

Josiah offered up a prayer of thankfulness. Then he sighed. He had saved Charlotte this time, but he knew that if they didn't get help soon, they would all starve.

Another Oppressed People

The Natives that Josiah and his family encountered most likely belonged to the Iroquois Confederacy, which included Iroquois, Huron, Algonkian and other tribes that lived around the Great Lakes. Although there were differences in language and customs between tribes, they shared many things in common. They were considered "woodland" peoples because they depended on forest products for their livelihood.

The Natives the Hensons met were likely frightened because they had never met Black people before. Perhaps the Natives' kindness to Josiah and his family stemmed in part from their understanding of what it was like to be dominated by white people. Soon after, the United States developed a policy to "civilize" the Natives so they would be like whites. This created a terrible tragedy that is still felt today.

Help From an Unexpected Source

The family were trudging along the road when Josiah saw four men approaching. His first thought was to hide, because they might be bounty hunters. Then he realized they were Natives. Josiah motioned for the others to be still, and he walked towards the men. As he neared, however, they started howling, then turned and fled.

Charlotte tugged at Josiah's arm. "They are going for more people so they can return and murder us."

"There were enough of them to kill us, if that's what they wanted," said Josiah. "It's too far for us to turn around and go back. We have to follow them."

As Hensons moved along the trail, they saw the Natives peeping at them from behind the trees. "Why, they are more frightened of us than we are of them," Josiah thought.

A few minutes later, they reached the Natives' wigwams and were met by a tall, stately man. "He must be their chief," thought Josiah. The man indicated to his people that the strangers were indeed human beings.

Now everyone crowded around. Some poked at the children, who jumped backwards with yelps of alarm. When the children jumped, so did the Natives. But soon they were all laughing together.

Using hand signals, Josiah told the chief where his family was going and what they needed. That night, the Hensons slept in a wigwam and feasted on meat roasted over an open fire. The next morning, they walked the last twenty-five miles to Sandusky City on the shore of Lake Erie, where Josiah planned to catch a boat to Canada.

At Last, Freedom!

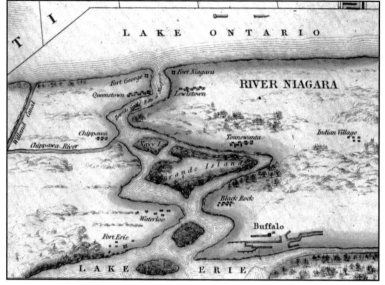

A nineteenth century map showing the border area between Canada and the United States, including Fort Erie

When they reached Sandusky, Josiah hid everyone in the woods while he ventured out to make arrangements. At the shore, he saw a group of men working on a boat. The captain saw him and called out, "Hello there, man! You want to work? I'll give you a shilling an hour."

"Yes, sir, I'll be happy to load your boat," said Josiah. He hoisted a bag of corn and carried it on board. "How far is it to Canada?" he asked a Black man working beside him.

"This boat is going to Buffalo, New York. Come along with us," the man said.

"How far is that from Canada?" asked Josiah.

"Just across the river."

Josiah decided that the man could be trusted. He told him about Charlotte and the children, who were waiting in the woods.

"Our captain's a fine fellow. He'll take you." The man left and returned a few minutes later with the captain.

"My wife and children are waiting in the woods," said Josiah.

The captain smiled. "I'll take you and your family to Buffalo. But it's best to wait until dark to bring them from the woods so the bounty hunters, who are always looking for escaped slaves, won't see them."

39

A Life of Spirituality

When Josiah Henson told the Captain that he would "give my soul to God," he made a promise that would affect the way he lived for the rest of his life. Josiah was a spiritual man who believed that everyone deserved to be free. His honesty and sense of fairness had kept him from escaping, because he felt that he owed his loyalty to his master. It was only when Riley tricked him and tried to "sell him South" that Josiah realized that protecting himself and his family was his most important concern. The compassion of the people who helped him during his escape, touched his soul. From that time on, Josiah devoted himself to aiding others, as others had assisted him and his family.

Later, when Josiah and his family returned to the boat, everyone on board welcomed them with three loud cheers.

"Come up on deck and clop your wings and craw like a rooster, because you're free!" said the captain.

Free! Josiah's happiness was so sharp, it felt like pain. After so much suffering and humiliation, they were at last with people who not only treated them like human beings, but rejoiced in their success at escaping from captivity. As the boat set sail, Josiah looked out over the moonlit water, and tears streamed down his cheeks.

When they reached Buffalo, the captain clapped Josiah on the shoulder. "See those trees," he said, pointing to a clump on shore, "they grow on free soil. As soon as your feet touch that, you're a man!" The next morning, he paid a boatman out of his own money to ferry the Hensons across the river into Canada. Then he put his hand on Josiah's head and said, "Be a good fellow, won't you?"

Josiah felt as if a lightning bolt had struck him. His entire body shook with emotion. "Yes," he said. "I will use my freedom well; I will give my soul to God."

The captain waved as the boat carrying the Hensons pushed away from shore. "God bless him," Josiah said to Charlotte. "God bless him eternally."

On the morning of October 28, 1830, Josiah Henson and his family stepped onto Canadian land in Fort Erie, Upper Canada, the area that would one day be Ontario. He threw himself on the ground, rolled in the sand, then stood and danced on the soil. He kissed Charlotte and hugged his children.

"He's some crazy fellow," said a nearby man.

"Oh, no, master!" Josiah laughed aloud. "Don't you know? I'm free!"

Josiah and family celebrate their arrival in a free country

A New Country

A Black settlement in southern Ontario. Often farmland had to be laboriously carved from the forest.

Being Black in Canada

Employers in Canada were happy to hire escaped slaves. For the slaves, earning a living wage that they could spend as they chose was like being reborn into a new life. In spite of these liberal attitudes, however, former slaves did encounter prejudice. In many places, Black children were not allowed to attend white schools. When Black farmers went to the mill to get their corn ground into meal, the mill owners refused to serve them. Josiah soon learned that, as a Black man, he had to succeed on his own. He dedicated himself to helping others do the same.

Josiah quickly set out to get work and find a place for his family to live. He learned of a Mr. Hibbard, who owned a large farm about eleven kilometres away from the town of Fort Erie. The farm had several shanties (run down houses) that Hibbard let out to the workers he hired. Josiah left his family in town, where they had found lodging for the night, and went to see Hibbard.

Hibbard hired Josiah and showed him a two-storey shanty where the Hensons could live. Josiah looked at the filthy floor, which several pigs had claimed as their home, and shuddered. As soon as Hibbard left, Josiah set to work. He put the pigs outside and, using a hoe, shovelled out the muck. Using many buckets of water, he scrubbed the floor until it was clean.

The next morning, Josiah fetched Charlotte and the children and brought them to their new home. Charlotte looked around the downstairs room and sighed.

"It's better than a log cabin with a dirt floor." She smiled up at her husband.

Josiah smiled back. After all their trials, they were at last in a home of their own. With straw that he got from Hibbard, Josiah made up beds—three foot high straw mats surrounded by logs—in every corner of the room. Then he, Charlotte and the children lay down to rest in the luxury of their own beds in their first home as free men and women. Never again would they fear being separated from those they loved.

42

Learning to Read

Josiah's Favourite Hymn

There is a land of pure delight,
Where saints immortal reign;
Infinite day excludes the night,
And pleasures banish pain.

There everlasting spring abides,
And never withering flowers:
Death, like a narrow sea, divides
This heav'nly land from ours.

Sweet fields beyond the swelling flood
Stand dressed in living green:
So to the Jews old Canaan stood,
While Jordan rolled between.

But timorous mortals start and shrink
To cross this narrow sea;
And linger, shivering on the brink,
And fear to launch away.

O could we make our doubts remove,
Those gloomy thoughts that rise,
And see the Canaan that we love
With unbeclouded eyes!

Could we but climb where Moses stood,
And view the landscape o'er,
Not Jordan's stream, nor death's cold flood,
Should fright us from the shore.

Like others before him, Hibbard appreciated Josiah's strength, honesty and work ethic. But Hibbard was an employer, not a master, and Josiah was a valued employee, not a slave. Mrs. Hibbard took a liking to the family and helped them get the things, such as pots and pans, furniture and clothing, that they needed to set up house. Soon the shanty became a real home.

Hibbard recognized that the Hensons' oldest son, Tom, was a bright boy and paid for him to go to school for two terms. The headmaster also recognized Tom's quick mind and love of learning and added more time. Tom was an eager student and was soon reading the books his teacher gave him.

A short time later, one of Josiah's friends from Maryland arrived in town. The two men greeted each other joyously, then the newcomer asked Josiah if he still preached sermons, as he had in Maryland.

"No, I don't," said Josiah.

His friend quickly spread the word that Josiah was an inspired preacher, and Josiah was soon addressing congregations, Black and white, throughout the area.

Now that Tom was literate, he often read to his father from the Bible. Tom was an inquisitive young man and peppered his father with questions. "Father, who was David?" he asked one Sunday.

Josiah had never heard of David. So he answered evasively, "He was a man of God, my son."

Tom responded, "I want to know something more about him. Where did he live? What did he do?" Tom looked at his father with sudden

awareness. "Why, Father, can't you read?"

Josiah lowered his eyes. "No, I cannot," he said.

"Why?" asked his son.

"Because I never had an opportunity."

Tom could not believe that his father, who preached so eloquently, could neither read nor write. Then and there, he offered to teach him, but Josiah declined. After all, he was fifty years old. How could he learn such a difficult skill at his age?

"I am too old and have not enough time. I must work all day, or you would not have enough to eat."

"No, Father. You must learn."

"But there is no one to teach me," said Josiah.

Tom looked at him and smiled. "I'll teach you, Father. You can do it. I know you can."

Tom began tutoring Josiah at night. They would read by the light of a burning pine knot or hickory bark, which was the only light they could afford. It was a frustrating task, both for father and son. Yet slowly, the squiggles that Tom showed Josiah began to take shape in his mind as sounds, and the sounds clumped together into words. As his reading skills improved, so did Josiah's appreciation of the depth of his enforced ignorance. And it made him more anxious than ever before to help those of his people who were still buried in the darkness of slavery. He ached for them, because he realized that they had no idea how degraded and lacking in knowledge they really were.

Conducting on the Underground Railroad

A famous painting showing abolitionists helping slaves on the Underground Railroad

"Those of us who have escaped to freedom are under obligation—first to God for our deliverance and secondly, to our fellow men—to do all that is in our power to bring others out of bondage." Josiah looked down at the faces turned up to him. He was preaching at a large meeting in Fort Erie, at which many Blacks were in attendance. As he stepped down from the podium, a well-dressed man, about his own age, approached him.

"Mr. Henson, please, may I speak with you?"

"Of course." Josiah motioned to a chair at the back of the room. They sat, and the other man introduced himself. "I'm James Lightfoot, and I was a slave on a plantation on the Ohio River, near the town of Maysville, Kentucky." He paused and wiped his face with a handkerchief. "I left my mother, father, three sisters and four brothers behind and, until today, I never thought about my duty to them. Now I realize how much I owe them. In my five years in Canada, I have accumulated some property. I am willing to commit it all and cooperate in any measure for my family's release." He looked at Josiah out of eyes filled with sadness. "Please, sir," he said, his voice cracking with emotion, "will you rescue them?"

The Quakers

Quakerism was started in England in the 1600s by people who were not happy with existing Christian churches. At that time, there was much religious persecution. One Quaker, William Penn, wanted to find a place where his people could live in freedom.

On March 4, 1681, King Charles II of England granted territory west of the Delaware River and north of Maryland to Penn. The King called the new colony Pennsylvania, meaning "Forests of Penn".

William Penn established a colony that offered freedom of religion. He granted women equal rights, gave the colony a written constitution which limited the power of government, provided a humane penal code, and guaranteed many fundamental liberties. Quakers opposed slavery, and many Quaker homes were "stations" on the Underground Railroad, where escaping slaves found shelter, food, friendship and encouragement.

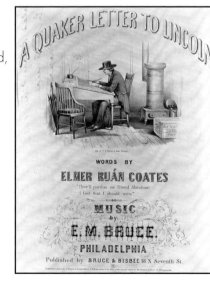

Josiah studied the man. He was obviously tortured by his failure to bring his family to the freedom he himself had found. What he was asking was momentous. He wanted Josiah to return to the South. Josiah knew he would be risking his own freedom, yet he too felt an obligation to those still in captivity. How could he refuse to help?

A few weeks later, Josiah set off on foot. Retracing the route he had taken on his own flight, he travelled four hundred miles until he reached the plantation where Lightfoot's people lived. Though delighted to see him and learn that their brother was safe, they claimed they were not ready to escape. The oldest Lightfoot brother explained. "Our parents are old and feeble; my sisters have many small children and, although I and my brothers can make the journey, we don't want to leave the others behind. However, if you return in one year, I promise we will go with you."

Josiah agreed to come back. He then travelled another forty miles, to Bourbon County in the interior of Kentucky, where he had heard that thirty people were prepared to escape. Once again, Josiah travelled at night and hid during the day. When he reached the group, he offered to lead them, and they were happy to accept.

Josiah and his "passengers" crossed the Ohio River and arrived in Cincinnati, where they rested for a few days. Their next stop was Richmond, Indiana, a town founded by Quakers (people opposed to slavery) who fed them, provided shelter and helped them on their way. Two weeks later, after a difficult trip through the Ohio wilderness, Josiah and his passengers reached the south-western shore of Lake Erie and booked passage on a boat to Canada.

A Second Trip on the Underground Railroad

Major routes of the Underground Railroad

Josiah returned home and spent the next summer working on his farm. Life was good. Charlotte was happy. By then the couple had had twelve children, of whom seven survived. Josiah's crops did well, and he continued to thank God every day for the miracle of his family's freedom.

That autumn, after the harvest was in, Josiah prepared to return to Maysville to keep his promise to rescue James Lightfoot's family.

By now, Josiah was an experienced Underground Railroad conductor. When he reached Portsmouth, Ohio, he knew that he had to take special precautions. Portsmouth was full of men from Kentucky who were ready to denounce any suspicious Black person.

Kentucky and Ohio

Kentucky was a slave state. Slaves who were caught trying to travel and whites who helped them were severely punished. If a ship's captain hired or took a fugitive slave on board, his ship could be seized and sold. Many slaves, from Kentucky and other slave states, tried to escape to neighbouring Ohio, a free state. For that reason, bounty hunters from Kentucky roamed around Ohio, looking for fugitive slaves.

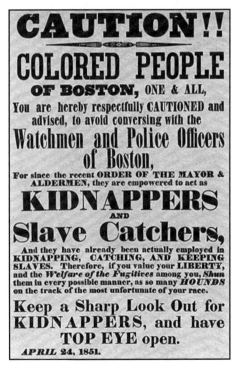

Even in "free" places like New England, former slaves had to be on their guard against slave catchers.

Josiah decided that his best hope was to make himself so ugly and disgusting that they would leave him alone. So he gathered dried leaves and wrapped them in a cloth which he tied around his face, nearly to his eyes. As he went through the town, he sputtered and made strange sounds, like a crazy person who could not speak.

"Who are you, boy?" A burly man with a grizzled beard and a fleshy nose stopped him as he walked down the main street.

Josiah shook his head and rolled his eyes.

"C'mon, boy, speak." The man brought his face so close to Josiah's that Josiah could smell his rancid breath. "Who owns ya? Where ya going?"

Josiah shook his head hard and let out a piercing wail.

The man stepped back, then shook his head and left.

As he walked away, Josiah went limp with relief.

A few days later, Josiah arrived in Maysville and almost immediately met James Lightfoot's brother Jefferson on the street.

"We're still determined to escape," Jefferson said, clapping Josiah on the shoulder.

"Good. We should do it next Saturday night," said Josiah. "That way you won't be missed until Monday, and by then we'll be a hundred miles away."

During the next few days, Josiah hid by day and met with the Lightfoot family at night. At the appointed time, Jefferson and his family crept away. They were so afraid of being detected that they left without saying goodbye to their parents.

48

A Desperate Decision

The house of Reverend John Rankin in Ohio just across from Kentucky, which was a slave state. It served as a safe house, or a "station" on the Underground Railroad for escaping slaves.

To avoid being caught by bloodhounds, Josiah and his party seized a small boat, which they paddled down the river. Suddenly one of the men screamed. "We're sinking."

Josiah spun around. Water was seeping through the floorboards as the boat sank lower and lower in the water.

"It's going down," he shouted. "We have to get to the shore."

One by one, the passengers slid into the river and began to swim. Luckily, they were only a short distance from the shore, and it seemed they would make it when the youngest Lightfoot boy called out that he couldn't move his legs.

"Hang on to me." The boy's brother grabbed him around the waist and paddled frantically until his feet touched the mud of the riverbank. By that time, the boy was shivering uncontrollably. Wrapping him in whatever clothing they had, Josiah and the men took turns carrying him.

The weather turned cold. Trudging through the woods, the party slogged through mud, rain and snow. On good days, they found refuge with Quaker families. The rest of the time, they slept in the open, covering themselves as best they could with their few pieces of clothing. Then one day, the boy who had almost drowned became violently ill.

The men took turns carrying him on their backs, and when this became too difficult, they fashioned a crude stretcher out of shirts and handkerchiefs laid across two wooden poles. In spite of their efforts, however, his condition worsened.

Harriet Tubman: The Underground Railroad's Most Famous Conductor

The Underground Railroad's most famous conductor was a former slave, Harriet Tubman. She made nineteen secret trips south and led over three hundred slaves to freedom. Many of them settled in and around St. Catharines, Ontario, where she lived at the time. Harriet travelled throughout Ontario to check up on the people she rescued. On these trips, she met and worked with Josiah Henson.

Tubman was so successful at rescuing slaves that she became known as "The Moses of her People". Plantation owners, however, considered her a threat and posted a $40,000 reward for her capture. During the Civil War, Harriet became a nurse and later a spy for the Union army. She and her troops destroyed plantations that were supplying food to the Confederate armies and freed over seven hundred and fifty slaves.

After the war, she used money raised by her supporters, along with funds from sales of her biography, to establish the Harriet Tubman Home for Aged and Indigent Negroes in Auburn, New York. In 1897, Harriet was honoured by England's Queen Victoria at the Queen's Diamond Jubilee celebrations. Harriet Tubman died on March 10, 1913, at the age of ninety-three.

"Leave me behind," the boy begged when they stopped to rest.

"We can't do that," his brother protested.

"You have to." The boy coughed until it seemed his frail ribs would crack. He caught his breath. "If you carry me through the bush, it will slow you down, and you might all be caught. I am going to die anyway, so leave me and save yourselves."

The Lightfoot family huddled together. How could they desert their brother? Yet, what choice did they have? Finally, after much soul-searching, they carried him to a secluded spot under some trees and made him as comfortable as possible.

They had gone about a mile when the boy's brother stopped and cried out. "I cannot do this! I cannot leave my brother to die alone in agony." Turning, he raced back along the trail with the rest of the party close on his heels. When they reached the young man, the whole family whooped with joy because he was still alive.

Once again they started their slow, perilous route through the woods. Josiah knew of other Underground Railroad conductors like Harriet Tubman, who had rescued many people under similar circumstances, and their success helped fuel his spirit. After a while, Josiah saw a wagon approaching from the opposite direction. He stepped into its path and waved. As the driver reined in his horses, Josiah ran up to him.

"Where is thee going?" The driver had kind blue eyes. His square brown beard and use of the word "thee" told Josiah that he was a Quaker.

"To Canada," said Josiah. "We have a very sick man with us."

Harriet Tubman

The Quaker motioned for them to get into the wagon.

The group spent the night with the Quaker family. The woman of the house fed them nourishing soups, meat and fresh baked bread. Then she showed them warm places where they could sleep. The next morning, as they prepared to be on their way, she stopped Josiah. "Leave the young one with us, and we will nurse him back to health."

The family agreed. The Quaker woman gave them a sack of biscuits and some meat, and, after bidding the kind family farewell, the group resumed their journey on the Underground Railroad, to Canada.

Slave Hunters

While travelling on the Underground Railroad, escaping slaves were always on the lookout for slave hunters, men who made a living catching fugitive slaves and returning them to their owners. Conductors learned ways of avoiding slave hunters.

Harriet Tubman was a master at avoiding slave hunters. Because newspapers didn't publish runaway-slave notices until Mondays, she spirited slaves away on Saturday nights, often using a slave owner's own wagon. When pursued by slave hunters, she would throw them off by suddenly turning south. To quiet babies, she used drugs to put them to sleep. Deeply spiritual but grimly determined, she threatened to shoot any "passenger" who dared to turn back. Later, she would proudly tell the great abolitionist Frederick Douglass that she "never lost a single passenger" on the Underground Railroad.

Frederick Douglass

A Narrow Escape

The group set out as before, hiding by day and walking through the woods at night, constantly on the lookout for the slave hunters who were stalking them. They had gone only a few miles when they met a white man who told them he was also on the run. "I'm a free man," he said, "but I attacked my employer because he mistreated me." The man joined their group and guided them on routes that would avoid the slave hunters.

They walked all night. In the morning, they stopped at an inn near the shore of Lake Erie and ordered breakfast. They were so exhausted that they all fell asleep at the table while waiting for their food.

Josiah awoke with a start. Something was wrong. He lifted his head and listened. A premonition tickled him, and though he was barely awake, he knew what he had to do. Jumping to his feet, he shook each of his companions awake. "We have to leave this house! Get up, get up," he begged.

Now everyone was awake. Following Josiah's lead, they jumped from their chairs, raced outside, and ducked behind a clump of bushes at the side of the road. They had barely hidden themselves when the thunder of horses' hooves filled the morning air.

"Slave hunters," whispered Jefferson Lightfoot.

Silently they watched as three men reined in their horses and dismounted. The leader stepped forward and pounded on the inn door. Josiah peered through the bushes and saw the door open and his white friend step outside. Josiah could hear the men talking but couldn't make out their words. Then his friend turned the slave hunter around and pointed west. A moment later, he and his companions jumped on their horses and rode off.

"What did you say to them?" Josiah asked when he returned to the inn.

"They asked whether I'd seen any slaves. So I told them yes." The man grinned. "I said there were six slaves, and they were all headed towards Detroit."

The landlord came over with the men's breakfast and Josiah told him what had happened. "If we had stayed in the house one more minute, we would have been discovered."

"I have a boat," the landlord said. "I'll take you in it to Canada. Now sit and eat."

The fugitives looked at him in disbelief and did as he said. After devouring their breakfast, they followed their host down to the lake. As they settled into the boat, Josiah felt as if his heart would explode with happiness. He looked at his companions and knew they were experiencing the same powerful emotion, marvelling at their incredible good luck.

When at last they reached the Canadian shore, the men leaped from the boat and danced and wept for joy. Then they lay on the ground and kissed the earth.

A few months later, Josiah returned to Ohio and brought the boy, now robust and healthy, to be reunited with his family in Canada. Soon after, the rest of the Lightfoot family which had remained in Kentucky joined them. Their owner, Frank Taylor, had suffered a nervous breakdown when he learned that his slaves had escaped. On his recovery, his friends had convinced him to set the rest of the family free.

After rescuing the Lightfoots, Josiah became a regular conductor on the Underground Railroad. He travelled to the South many times and led 118 slaves to freedom.

The British American Manual Labour Institute

The Dawn Community

Once Josiah had established his family, he turned to the plight of other escaped slaves. He and his friend Hiram Wilson called together a group of former slaves and sympathizers. They met in London, Upper Canada in 1838 and agreed to build a school.

After the meeting, Josiah and Wilson looked for a suitable site, settling on two hundred acres on the Sydenham River in the town of Dawn. Josiah moved his family to Dawn in 1842, and the town became a prosperous Black community.

At its height, the Dawn settlement included a sawmill, cornmill, brickyard and the school that provided Black students with a general education. About five hundred people lived on the land. Most were farmers who exported their crops, along with local black walnut lumber, to the U.S. and England. In his commitment to the settlement, Josiah realized his goal of encouraging former slaves to become skilled labourers and self-sufficient.

Josiah Henson in the 1850s

Josiah believed that education was the path to true freedom. He asked the Reverend Hiram Wilson for help. Wilson, who had been sent to Canada in 1836 by the American Anti-Slavery Society to help Canadian Blacks, contacted James C. Fuller, a Quaker and philanthropist who lived in Skaneateles, New York. Fuller traveled to England, where he raised $1500 from English Quakers.

Henson called a meeting of the most successful former slaves living in Upper Canada to decide what to do with the money Fuller had raised. He wanted to build a manual labour school to educate Black children in the basics they needed to succeed on their own. Although fugitive slaves were welcomed into Canada, there was still prejudice against them attending school with white children. Josiah proposed that, in addition to the basic tools of literacy, boys would be taught manual labour skills and the girls "those domestic arts which are the proper occupations of their sex."

The committee used the money Fuller had raised to purchase two hundred acres of land on the Sydenham River, in today's southwestern Ontario. In 1842, they built the school, which they named the British American Manual Labour Institute, and a sawmill. Josiah moved his family to Dawn.

54

The 1851 World's Fair

The Great Exhibition of 1851 in England was the very first World's Fair. Visitors saw exhibits of the greatest inventions of the 1800s. Photography, which was still very new, was showcased as a major attraction. The centrepiece of the fair was the Crystal Palace, a gigantic modular building made of glass and steel.

He then travelled throughout New York, Connecticut, Massachusetts, and Maine to raise money for the school.

At first the sawmill did well, but eventually the joint operation of the mill and school ran up a debt of $7500. The committee decided to separate the two, and Josiah took over responsibility for managing the mill. He went to England to raise money, carrying with him letters of recommendation from prominent people in the United States who were supporters of the school.

Josiah had only raised $1700 when rumours began circulating in England that he was an imposter. He agreed to return to Canada with an agent, John Scoble, to clear his name. They succeeded, and Scoble went back to England, leaving money in trust for Henson's passage, should he ever want to return.

By this time, the Dawn students were producing beautiful, highly polished wood boards from the black walnut trees that grew in the area and turning them into beautiful furniture. In 1851, Josiah decided to use Scoble's money to take his students' work to exhibit at the Great Exhibition being held in England.

The Crystal Palace, an engineering marvel of its time, was the centrepiece of the 1851 World's Fair.

Josiah Meets the Queen

Exhibitors at the World's Fair

Although people from all over Europe, Asia, and America took part in the London World's Fair, Josiah Henson was the only Black exhibitor. Josiah was saddened to see Blacks from Africa who were brought to the fair and exhibited like exotic animals. He hoped that sometime soon, other Black people, like himself, would be exhibiting on their own behalf.

Queen Victoria

When he got to the exhibition, Josiah found that, because he had shipped his products on an American ship, they were being exhibited at the American Pavilion. He objected. "I am a citizen of Canada, my boards are from Canada, and there is a section in this building devoted to Canadian products."

The American in charge told him, "You can exhibit what belongs to you if you please, but not a single thing here must be moved an inch without my consent."

Furious, Josiah decided that if he couldn't move his items, at least he would tell the world who had made them. He hired a printer to paint a sign saying, "This is the product of the industry of a Fugitive Slave from the United States, whose residence is Dawn, Canada."

The American was upset, but the people crowding into the exhibit were delighted. Perhaps it was Josiah's black complexion that attracted their attention, or their own reflections in the large colour mirrors, but virtually everyone who walked by stopped at his booth. One of these people was Queen Victoria. The Queen paused to look at Josiah and his products. He uncovered his head and saluted her.

As she left, Josiah overheard her say, "Is he indeed a fugitive slave?"

One of her aides answered, "He is indeed, and that is his work."

An example of a black walnut chair made at the Dawn Settlement

Josiah made enough money to cancel the school's debts, but he was called home because his wife Charlotte was seriously ill. A short time later, Josiah received a package from England. In it were a bronze medal for his students' work, and a framed picture of the Queen and the royal family for himself.

On his return from London, Josiah also found that problems had arisen with the sawmill. At first it had been profitable. Its location on the River Sydenham had allowed the lumber to be shipped to Detroit or any port in the United States. The sawmill was leased to a man who employed about fifty men. After three good years, however, the mill ran into financial difficulties. The man who had leased it loaded all the lumber onto three boats and sailed off, leaving his workmen starving and without money. When he didn't return, the workmen, in anger, destroyed the mill. Josiah felt as if he had lost a dear friend.

A replica of the sawmill at the Dawn settlement

Starting Over

Josiah and his second wife Nancy in 1877,
twenty years after their marriage

Charlotte died soon after Josiah's return from London. He was desolate. They had been married for fifty years. She had lived with him as a slave, escaped to freedom with him and had helped him forge a new life in Canada. Josiah did not know how he could carry on without her.

For the next four years, as he continued working his farm and preaching, he mourned for Charlotte. But he was lonely. So in 1855, he went to Boston to visit a woman he had met, with whom he felt he would be happy. Nancy Gambrid was a widow; a free Black woman with one son and two daughters. She had been raised in Baltimore by a Quaker family and was well-educated. Her mother had been a slave but had earned enough money as a laundress to buy her own and her husband's freedom.

Josiah called on Nancy several times before summoning the courage to ask her to marry him. She agreed, and they were married in Boston two years later. Nancy moved to Canada with Josiah.

Josiah's Autobiography

Josiah had one surviving brother who was a slave on a farm in Maryland. His brother was so demoralized by slavery that he lacked the resolve to escape. On his return from England, Josiah found out that his brother's owner would give him manumission papers for $400. Josiah decided to write his life story in order to raise the money to buy his brother's freedom. His anti-slavery friends in Boston agreed to publish it.

Once it was printed, Josiah took the books and sold them himself. He raised the money and ransomed his brother, bringing him to Dawn. The brother later moved back to the United States and lived as a free man.

The cover of a later edition of Josiah's autobiography

Uncle Tom's Cabin: The Book that Started a War

When Josiah Henson met the writer Harriet Beecher Stowe on one of his preaching trips to Massachusetts, he was impressed by her compassion and her desire to learn of his life as a slave. Mrs. Stowe had read his life story *(The Life of Josiah Henson, Formally a Slave, Now an Inhabitant of Canada)* a book he had published in 1849 to raise money to buy his brother John's freedom. She said she hoped it would open people's eyes to the evils of slavery. In 1852, she published her own book, *Uncle Tom's Cabin,* which became an immediate success. People read it openly in the North and in secret in the South. When some accused her of exaggerating the cruelty of slavery, she pointed to Josiah Henson's book as proof that these horrors did exist. From that time on, Josiah became known as "Uncle Tom", a title he said he was proud to wear, but one which caused him many problems over the years.

Slavery was becoming an increasingly bitter issue between the northern and southern states. *Uncle Tom's Cabin* told the story of one plantation where the slaves were mistreated by a cruel overseer, Simon Legree, much like the man, Bruce Litton, who had broken Josiah's arm and crippled him for life. As Josiah's fame spread, he was asked to speak to groups all over the North, to try and turn public sentiment in favour of abolishing slavery.

Tension between the North and South had been building for many years, with slavery as a key issue.

Uncle Tom's Cabin
and The Civil War

Uncle Tom's Cabin was the best-selling novel of the 19th century. In the year after it was published, it sold 300,000 copies in the United States alone. When United States President Abraham Lincoln met Stowe during the Civil War, he was quoted as saying "So this is the little lady who made this big war."

The end of slavery did not, however, end prejudice against Black people. Jim Crow laws in the South prohibited them from attending white schools. Blacks could not swim in public swimming pools, drink from the same water fountains or use the same washrooms as whites. They had to sit in the back of public buses and give up their seat if a white person wanted it. It would be another hundred years, in the Civil Rights movement in the 1960s, before blacks demanded, and got, the equality and civil rights they had been promised.

When anti-slavery president Abraham Lincoln took power, eleven southern states left the union and formed their own government, the Confederate States of America. A Civil War broke out on April 12, 1861, when the Confederacy fired on the Union's Fort Sumter in South Carolina.

Many Blacks in Canada wanted to fight with the North to help free slaves. Josiah was too old to enlist but encouraged others to do so. His son-in-law Wheeler enlisted in Detroit, and his eldest son Tom, who had gone to California, enlisted on a ship in San Francisco. Josiah never heard from him again and assumed he was dead.

The war lasted for four years. It ended on April 9, 1865, when Robert E. Lee, the southern commander, surrendered to northern general Ulysses S. Grant. It was the bloodiest war in the history of the United States, with thousands of soldiers and civilians killed on each side.

Robert E. Lee

Ulysses S. Grant

This contemporary propaganda illustration shows a former slave's journey from the fields to being a free Union soldier, and eventually a martyr for the United States.

The Emancipation Proclamation

On January 1, 1863, when the United States was in the third year of the Civil War, President Lincoln issued a proclamation stating that "all persons held as slaves" within the rebel states "are, and henceforward shall be free." The Proclamation did not free slaves in the border states like Maryland and Kentucky. It only freed them in the states that had broken away from the Union. However, it committed the U.S. to end slavery, which it did, in every state that it conquered. Once the war was over, abolitionists pushed for an amendment to the constitution to permanently end slavery. The 13th Amendment was ratified on December 18, 1865.

The Henson Family

After the Civil War, Josiah continued preaching and working on his farm in Dawn, and he remained involved in the affairs of his community. As a Methodist Episcopal elder, he had a district of three hundred miles. He travelled, held meetings, attended conferences, established churches and was involved in "every movement that has been started for the improvement of our people."

Josiah took pride in his children. Two died young, including Tom, who was assumed killed in the Civil War. His second son, Isaac was educated in London, with the help of Josiah's friends. He married and was ordained as a Wesleyan minister. When he died at the age of thirty-seven, he was well-loved and respected. The Hensons' third son, Josiah, wanted to become a shoemaker. At twenty-two, he married and moved to Jackson, Michigan, where he found great prejudice in the shoe business against hiring a Black person. As his father before him, he found help from an Englishman, a boot and shoemaker who took him on as an apprentice. After two years, he opened his own business. Josiah's fourth son, Peter, became a

This illustration celebrates the Emancipation Proclamation of 1863

Excerpt from a Letter by Thomas Hughes, Missionary of the Church of England, Dresden

...For many years he [Josiah Henson] was a slave, and was most cruelly treated. Since his escape to Canada, now more than forty years ago, he has occupied a foremost place in all movements for the advancement of his people. Through his efforts for their good he has, unfortunately, suffered considerable pecuniary [financial] loss, and has been compelled in consequence to mortgage his farm. It is with the view of lifting this incumbrance that he has, in his extreme old age, resolved, in response to a cordial invitation given him, to visit England. I heartily commend him and his cause to the British public and hope that he may have, in every respect, a prosperous journey by the will of God.

farmer and helped his father run the family farm. His four daughters were all married and literate, a source of great pride to their father, who had struggled to learn to read and write.

One problem continued to plague Josiah—the legal debts he owed from seven years of lawsuits involving ownership of the Dawn property.

At the suggestion of Reverend Thomas Hughes, the Secretary of the Colonial and Continental Missionary Church Society in Canada, Josiah decided to return to London, England. Hughes wrote a letter to his friends suggesting they help Josiah raise the money to pay off his debts. So, armed with letters from friends in Canada, Josiah and Nancy left for London in the spring of 1876.

A Visit to Windsor Castle

Josiah was excited to be back in London, seeing again the people who had been his friends for so many years. He was still an imposing figure, tall with a head of snowy white hair and a full beard to match. In an article for the weekly paper *Christian Age,* Josiah's friend, Professor Fowler, described him. "Though in his eighty-eighth year, he appears to be at least fifteen years younger. Uncle Tom, at eighty-eight, is buoyant, elastic and still anxious to make improvements."

Josiah's meeting with the Queen

A highlight of the Hensons' London stay was a trip to Windsor Castle, where they had an audience with Queen Victoria. Her Majesty said that she had been acquainted with Josiah's history for many years and presented him with her photograph, signed 'Victoria Reg., 1877.'

Josiah thanked her for "the great honour conferred upon himself, as well as on behalf of his coloured brethren in Canada and other portions of her Majesty's dominions—for her august protection when they were poor fugitive slaves."

By the time the Hensons left London, Josiah had collected enough money to pay off all his debts so, as his friends had wished, he and Nancy could live out their lives in comfort, free from want.

An illustration from an edition of
Uncle Tom's Cabin

**This poem was published in the
Birmingham Daily Mail, on March 6, 1877.**

A Negro Preacher, bowed with age, is he:
No sounding titles do his worth attest,
Yet, in a land where all who tread are free,
He, slave who was, is now its Sov'rein's guest!
What deep emotion must possess his breast,
The humble actor in so strange a scene!
Once all unknown, unfriended, and opprest,
He who a legal "chattel" erst had been,
In friendly converse stands with England's gracious Queen!

What wonder if, amid that courtly throng,
His startled thoughts fly back through years of pain,
When held in cruel bonds by foulest wrong,
Condemned to labour for a tyrant's gain,
He felt the lash, and wore the captive's chain—

Hunted by hounds, when fain he would be free;
Accursed, as though he bore the brand of Cain;
Like some wild beast, from men
compelled to flee,
In desperate essay to snatch sweet Liberty!

Brave "Uncle Tom!" May happy days be thine—
Days placid, peaceful, uneventful, still!
May tender friendships sweeten thy decline!
As flow'rets fringe the homeward-flowing rill,
May love they fleeting years with comfort fill—
The Master whom thou lovest doth accord
True freedom unto all who do his will;
And, in the service of their common Lord,

Both Queen and slave at last shall reap a rich reward.

An Uncle Tom

Josiah's notoriety as the real "Uncle Tom" was a mixed blessing. It helped him raise money for his school and other causes. Yet many people thought of the "Uncle Tom" in Stowe's book as a person who would do anything to please his white masters. Being called an "Uncle Tom" often was (and still is) considered an insult.

Was Josiah an "Uncle Tom"? He spent many years doing Riley's bidding, and he never forgave himself for not freeing Riley's slaves when he had the chance. Yet once he escaped, Josiah became an outspoken abolitionist and used his friendships with whites to help his own people. He was proud that Harriet Beecher Stowe used him as the prototype for her book, but he spent the rest of his life proving that he was not the kind of "Uncle Tom" that many people thought of as a traitor to his people.

Harriet Beecher Stowe

Uncle Tom's Farewell Meeting

While in England, Josiah preached to many congregations. On January 30, 1877, he held his last meeting before returning to Canada. Nearly six thousand people filled the Spurgeon's Metropolitan Tabernacle in London. Josiah's renown had made him a star—a person others wanted to see and hear speak. People crowded the tabernacle floor and galleries, anxious to hear the words of the man they knew as "Uncle Tom". After a service led by the Reverend J.A. Spurgeon, Josiah spoke for over an hour. At the conclusion of his speech, he delighted his audience by singing "The Slaves' Parting Hymn", a song sung by thousands of slaves when they were about to be bought, sold and separated from the people they loved.

My brethren fare ye well,
I do you now tell,
I'm sorry to leave you,
I love you so well.

I shortly must go,
And where I don't know;
Wherever I'm stationed
The trumpet I'll blow.

Strange people I'll find;
I hope they'll prove kind;
Neither place nor faces
Shall alter my mind.

Wherever I'll be,
I'll still pray for thee;
And you, my dear brethren,
Do the same for poor me.

Josiah Visits His Old Home in Maryland

The Original "Uncle Tom's" Cabin

The Maryland house on the plantation where Josiah Henson spent his youth was purchased by Montgomery County, Maryland, and is being preserved as an historic site. On June 24, 2006, the day it was first shown to the public, tour guide Warren Fleming told visitors about how his great-great-grandfather had been enslaved on a Montgomery County plantation, and how proud he was to guide the first tours inside Josiah's old home.

"Uncle Tom is America. This cabin tells us where we were and where we have to go," said Fleming. "This is something for our kids. When they're brought up today, they don't know this kind of history, they don't know what it was to be a slave in Maryland."

The winter after his return from England, Josiah experienced a powerful urge to visit his boyhood home in Maryland. His wife, who was from Baltimore, was anxious to see her married sister, who lived there.

The Hensons arrived in Baltimore on December 26, 1877, and stayed with Nancy's family until March 3, 1878. Then they went to Washington D.C., where they were welcomed by President Rutherford B. Hayes at the White House. As he had in England, Josiah marvelled at the strange fate that saw him, a former slave, accepted as an equal by one of the most powerful men in the world

The Hensons' next stop was Josiah's old home, the Riley plantation, which Josiah had not seen in over fifty years.

As their buggy approached the farm, Josiah's spirits fell. The great plantation of his youth was now a wilderness of dead trees and neglected, weed-choked fields. The house they had called the Great House was run down and badly in need of repair.

As they drove up, a young Black boy came out and stared at them.

"Does Mrs. Riley live here?" Josiah asked.

"Yes, sir."

"Can she be seen?"

"Dunno, sir; she's poorly and isn't out of bed today." The boy went inside, and a moment later bid the Hensons to come into the house.

Josiah found his old mistress in bed in what used to be the sitting room. It was the first place that looked familiar, although the furniture was

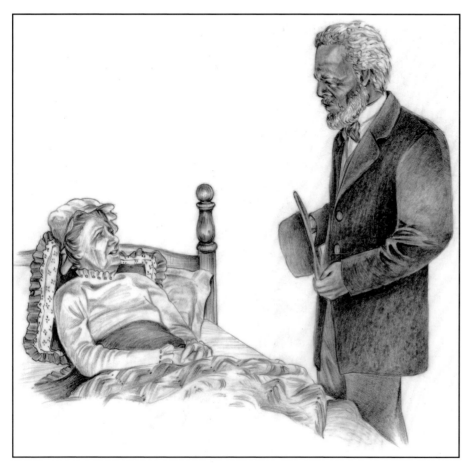

worn and the floor bare of carpets. He went up to Mrs. Riley and bowed. "How do you do, Madam?"

"I'm poorly—poorly. How do you do? I don't seem to know you."

The woman peered up at Josiah. Suddenly, she sprang up in bed. "Can it be Si? It is Si! Oh, Si, your poor master is dead and gone!"

Josiah shook his head. "No, Madam. My master is alive."

She leaned forward, squinting to get a better look at him. "Why, Si, you are a gentleman."

Josiah smiled. "I always was, Madam."

She began to question him, asking for the names of officers under whom Mr. Riley had served in the war of 1812. To her great delight, Josiah was able to name them all. Her son-in-law, who had come into the room, wrote them down.

"She needs the names so she can claim her husband's army pension," he explained. "They won't give it to her without proper accreditation."

"I'm glad I can help." Josiah looked at Mrs. Riley, reduced to such a sad state, and sighed. "I hope she gets the money. I see that she can use it."

A Final Farewell

Josiah Henson's great-grandchildren Thelma and Tom in the 1960s with Jack Thomson, curator of the Henson house, at Henson's grave site in Dresden, Ontario.

Josiah turned to Mrs. Riley's son-in-law. "Before I leave, there is one thing I would like to do. I wish to see my mother's grave."

"You take him," Mrs. Riley said to her son-in-law.

Josiah said goodbye to his former mistress and followed her son-in-law out of the house. They walked in silence across the yard to a collection of grass covered mounds. When they reached his mother's grave, Josiah lay on top of it, hid his face in the grass and wept. He wept for the woman who had spent her life as a slave, and for all the slaves who had suffered on this plantation and throughout the South.

When his tears were spent, Josiah stood, brushed the grass from his clothes, and bid his old home a silent goodbye. Then he and Nancy returned to their buggy and left the Riley plantation behind.

Josiah and Nancy returned to Dawn, where he continued to preach, write and lecture until his death in 1883 at the age of ninety-three.

Uncle Tom's Cabin Historic Site

Uncle Tom's Cabin Historic Site

Two People Behind Uncle Tom's Cabin Historic Site

Barbara Carter, Josiah's great-great granddaughter, has been aware of her famous relative and his legacy all her life. Barbara was born and raised in Dresden, Ontario, on former British American Institute property where the memory of the slaves who found freedom in Canada remains fresh. She married, had three daughters, and after they were grown, she became involved in preserving Josiah's life history. Barbara was instrumental in starting the Uncle Tom's Cabin Historic Site Advisory Committee. She was Site Manager for fifteen years, and helped to guide the site's direction.

Steven Cook was also born and raised in Dresden. As a young person, he became interested in Josiah's story and volunteered at the site as a teenager. While a student at university, he spent his summers as an intern, and after graduation began working there. Together he and Barbara are committed to promoting Josiah's legacy through education and outreach to the Canadian and international communities.

Although the Dawn Settlement is long gone, its history and legacy have been preserved. The Uncle Tom's Cabin Historic Site in Dresden, Ontario, sits on five acres of land that were part of the original two hundred acres that Josiah and his supporters bought in 1841. William Chappel, a local resident, bought the property in the 1940s. In 1948, he moved the house 150 feet, to separate it from his own home, and opened it to visitors. Jack Thomson bought the house in 1964 and turned it into a museum. In 1967 he opened the Henson House, Church and Harris House to visitors. He added a gift shop, entrance and built a museum behind the gift shop.

Thomson remained active in running the museum until 1984, when he sold it to the County of Kent. Kent County operated it until 1992, when they sold it to the St. Clair Parks commission, which then set up an advisory committee to guide the museum's development with the help of a $1.2 million capital grant from the Ontario Ministry of Tourism. Money from the grant was used to restore the Henson and Harris houses and the church and to build the new Interpretive Centre, which opened in the spring of 1996. There are five historic sites.

• The Harris House, where fugitive slaves sought refuge, is one of the oldest structures in the area. The Smokehouse, housed in the trunk of a sycamore tree, was once used for preserving meat.

• The Sawmill represents one of the methods used to clear the land. Profits went to support the British American Institute that Josiah founded to train former slaves in marketable skills.

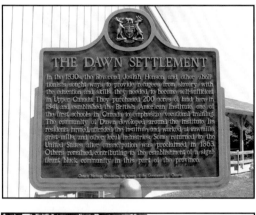

Josiah
Henson's
pulpit

• The Josiah Henson House is the dwelling where Josiah Henson and his second wife Nancy lived during the latter part of his life. In 1993-94, the home was restored to the way it looked in 1850.

• The Pioneer Church, which dates back to 1850, contains the organ from the original church where Henson preached in Dresden, Ontario. His pulpit and his church's sign are on display in the Underground Railroad Freedom Gallery.

• The Henson Family Cemetery is located next to the church. The Josiah Henson memorial stone and National Historic Plaque are located here (see page 69). Across the road is the British American Institute burial ground where many gravestones of the settlement have been preserved.

Visitors to the Interpretive Centre are first ushered into the North Star Theatre, where they watch a video, *Father Henson: His Spirit Lives On.* Next they go to the Underground Railroad Freedom Gallery, to view exhibits about the history of freedom seekers, from the time they were captured in Africa and enslaved in the United States to their escape to freedom in Canada. The Centre also houses a collection of artifacts from the 1800s, rare books, including an early edition of Josiah's autobiography, and the signed photo of Queen Victoria presented to Josiah in 1877.

The Ontario Heritage Trust took over the property in 2005 and runs it today.

Since his death, Josiah has been recognized as a true Canadian hero. In 1983, he became the first Black person to be featured on a Canadian stamp. In 1999, he was recognized by the Historic Sites and Monuments Board of Canada as a National Historic Person. This federal plaque to him is located in the Henson family cemetery, next to Uncle Tom's Cabin Historic Site.

JOSIAH HENSON
(1789 – 1883)

After escaping to Upper Canada from slavery in Kentucky, the Reverend Josiah Henson became a conductor of the Underground Railroad and a force in the abolition movement. The founder of the Black settlement of Dawn, he was also an entrepreneur and established a school, the British-American Institute. His fame grew after Harriet Beecher Stowe stated that his memoirs published in 1849 had provided "conceptions and incidents" for her extraordinarily popular novel, *Uncle Tom's Cabin*. Henson's celebrity raised international awareness of Canada as a haven for refugees from slavery.

Après s'être enfui du Kentucky où il vivait en esclavage, le révérend Henson s'installa au Haut-Canada et s'imposa comme chef de file dans le réseau du chemin de fer clandestin et au sein du mouvement abolitionniste. Fondateur de la communauté noire de Dawn, il fut aussi un entrepreneur et mit sur pied une école, le British-American Institute. Il devint particulièrement célèbre quand Harriet Beecher Stowe déclara s'être inspirée de ses mémoires, publiés en 1849, pour écrire son célèbre roman *La Case de l'oncle Tom*. La renommée de Henson révéla au monde que le Canada s'avérait une terre d'accueil pour les esclaves fugitifs.

Historic Sites and Monuments Board of Canada
Commission des lieux et monuments historiques du Canada

Government of Canada · Gouvernement du Canada   1999

Josiah Henson's Life and Times

mid 1400s	Western Europeans begin to capture and enslave African people.
1500s-1800s	Millions of slaves are transported to European colonies in the New World.
1619	First Africans arrive in Jamestown, Virginia.
1641	Massachusetts Bay Colony legalizes slavery.
1642	Virginia passes a law making it illegal to help runaway slaves.
1660	Maryland and Virginia pass laws legalizing slavery of Africans.
1740	North Carolina makes it legal to prosecute people who help slaves to escape.
1755	The thirteen American colonies recognize slavery as legal.
1770s	Slavery becomes economically important in the plantation system of growing tobacco, rice, sugar cane and indigo.
1775	The first abolitionist society is founded in Philadelphia.
1776	The American Revolution begins.
1787	The new United States constitution forbids Congress from interfering with the slave trade.
1789	***Josiah Henson is born.***
1793	Canada passes an anti-slavery law.
1794	*Henson's father is beaten and sold. Josiah, his mother and five siblings are returned to his mother's owner, Dr. McPherson.*
1797	*Dr. McPherson dies, and the Hensons are sold. Josiah is reunited with his mother when his new owner sells him to her new owner.*
1793	The U.S. Congress passes the First Fugitive Slave Act.
1804	Slavery is abolished in most of the northern states.
1808	U.S. Congress makes it illegal to import African slaves.
1811	*Josiah and Charlotte are married.*
1825	*Josiah takes Riley's slaves to Amos Riley in Kentucky.*
1829	*Riley cheats Josiah on his manumission agreement.*
1830s	A network to help escaping slaves is called the Underground Railroad, after the growing network of railroad trains.
1830	The American Anti-Slavery Society is founded by Lewis Tappan. Vigilance committees in northern cities prevent return of escaped slaves to the south.
1830	*Josiah and his family escape to Canada.*
1833	The British Emancipation Act abolishes all slavery in the British Empire. This includes Canada.
1841	*Josiah moves his family to Dresden, Ontario and helps establish the Dawn Settlement.*
1842	*Josiah is instrumental in establishing the British American Institute.*
1840s	*Josiah Henson is a conductor on the Underground Railroad.*

1849	Harriet Tubman escapes from slavery in Maryland. Over the next fifteen years, she leads hundreds of other slaves to freedom.
1849	*Josiah Henson publishes his autobiography.*
1850	Congress passes the Second Fugitive Slave Act, making Canada the safest destination for an escaped slave.
1851	*Josiah takes his students' work to the World's Fair in London. He is called home when Charlotte becomes ill.*
1850	The Second Fugitive Slave Act is passed by U.S. Congress.
1852	Harriet Beecher Stowe publishes *Uncle Tom's Cabin.*
1852	*Charlotte Henson dies.*
1857	*Josiah marries Nancy Gambrid.*
1860	Abraham Lincoln is elected president of the United States.
1861	The Civil War breaks out between the slave-holding Southern States (the Confederacy) and the free Northern States (the Union). *Josiah suspends his Underground Railroad activities.*
1863	U.S. president Abraham Lincoln issues the Emancipation Proclamation, freeing the slaves.
1865	The Civil War ends when the Confederacy surrenders.
1865	The Thirteenth Amendment to the U.S. Constitution prohibits slavery.
1866	The Fourteenth Amendment extends civil rights to all former slaves.
1869	The Fifteenth Amendment permits men to vote without regard to race, colour or previous slave status.
1876	*Josiah and Nancy make their last trip to London where he meets Queen Victoria.*
1877	*Josiah visits his old home in Maryland and meets with President Rutherford B. Hayes in the White House.*
1883	*Josiah Henson dies at the age of ninety-three.*

About the Author

As a writer and editor for over thirty years, Rona Arato has written on a wide variety of subjects. Her work has appeared in magazines and newspapers in Canada, the United States and England. Rona is the author of *Fossils, Clues to Ancient Life, World of Water* (Crabtree, 2004), *Ice Cream Town* (Fitzhenry and Whiteside, 2007) and *Courage and Compassion: Ten Canadians Who Made a Difference* (Maple Tree Press, 2008).

She and her husband Paul moved to Toronto in 1970, where she began writing while raising her three children. She has written educational materials for organizations including Mosdos Press in Cleveland, Girl Guides of Canada, and B'nai Brith Canada.

From 1994-1998, Rona had the privilege of serving as an interviewer for *Survivors of the Shoa,* a Steven Spielberg project that recorded the histories of Holocaust survivors. It was this experience that fostered her interest in writing about human rights. Rona discovered Josiah Henson's story while researching a project on Canadian heroes and was taken with his strength and courage in the face of seemingly insurmountable obstacles.

Acknowledgements

Many people have helped make this book a reality. I am indebted to Steven Cook, Site Manager of the Uncle Tom's Cabin Historic Site and Barbara Carter, Josiah Henson's great-great-granddaughter, for their help and valuable insights in Josiah's life and legacy, and to the Ontario Heritage Fund for allowing us to use archival photos. Thank you to Anne Fothergill of the Montgomery County Department of Parks and Planning for allowing me to tour the "Uncle Tom's Cabin" site in Rockville, Maryland, before it was officially opened to the public.

I want to thank my husband Paul for his constant support and encouragement. To the writing group: Anne Dublin, Sydell Waxman, Lynn Westerhout and Frieda Wishinsky, who read, re-read and then read the manuscript once again, your encouragement and editing skills are invaluable.

Special thanks to the wonderful group at Napoleon & Company: Sylvia McConnell, who shares my vision of Josiah Henson; my editor, Allison Thompson, and Chrissie Wysotski, whose tender drawings bring the story to life.

Thank you to the Canada Council for the Arts, the Ontario Arts Council, and the Toronto Arts Council for their financial support during the writing of this book. Their recognition added validity to my quest to celebrate Josiah Henson and his heroic life.

The majority of the dialogue in this book is quoted directly from Josiah Henson's autobiography. The author has taken some license in certain scenes for narrative purposes.

Index

Resources

Autobiography of Josiah Henson by Josiah Henson (Dover Publications Inc., 1969)

Hidden in Plain View by Jacqueline L. Tobin and Raymond G. Dobard, Ph.D. (Anchor Books, 2000)

Extracts from Queen Victoria's Journal, Royal Archives, Windsor Castle

INTERNET RESOURCES

Dictionary of Canadian Biography Online, Library and Archives Canada
www.biographi.ca

The African American Registry®
www.aaregistry.com/african_american_history/954/Josiah_Henson_a_true_abolitionist

Ontario Heritage Trust
www.heritagefdn.on.ca

Hartgrove, W.B., "The Story of Josiah Henson"
Journal of Negro History 3 (January 1918) 1-21
http://dinsdoc.com/hartgrove-1.htm

Jumping the Broom—Wikipedia, the free encyclopedia
http://en.wikipedia.org/wiki/Jumping_the_broom

Uncle Tom's Cabin Historic Site
http://www.uncletomscabin.org

Slavery in America
http://www.slaveryinamerica.org

The Freedom Trail
http://www.freedomtrail.ca

Photo and Art Credits

Illustrations by Chrissie Wysotski
    Cover, pages a6, 7, 11, 16, 18, 23, 26, 28, 29, 33 ,37, 44, 53, 68

Library of Congress, Prints and Photographs Division (digital identification numbers)
    1 (3a42003), 2 (13305), 3 (2033), 4 (31930), 8 (3c24831), 13 (3a10460), 14
    (3g04550), 17 (3c27759), 19 (3g05321), 22 (3c16045), 27 (3b23576), 28
    (4a13377), 30 (3g02284), 45 (3a29554), 46 (3a15297), 49 (129166), 51
    (3a10453), 60 (3a05520), 61 (05453), 62 (3a06245), 65 (1184), 66 (3a13608)

Library and Archives Canada
    38 (C-000053), 42 (C-011811)

Rona Arato
    9, 20, 67

Uncle Tom's Cabin Historic Site, Dresden, Ontario
    10, 39, 41, 64, 69, 72

Sylvia McConnell
    57, 71

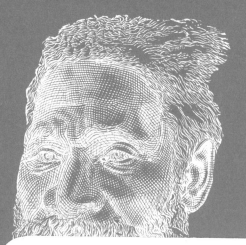